ARSÈNE LUPIN

The Stage Play

SHERLOCK HOLMES

Arsène Lupin vs. Sherlock Holmes
The Stage Play

by
Victor Darlay
&
Henry de Gorsse

based on characters created
by
Maurice Leblanc
and
Sir Arthur Conan Doyle

adapted in English
by
Frank J. Morlock

A Black Coat Press Book

Acknowledgements: We are indebted to Jackie Stanton for typing the plays and David McDonnell for proofreading the typescript.

This book is dedicated to Gerry Tetrault for a lifetime of friendship.

Arsène Lupin created by Maurice Leblanc.
Sherlock Holmes created by Sir Arthur Conan Doyle.

Visit our website at www.blackcoatpress.com

Table of Contents

Arsène Lupin vs. Sherlock Holmes

Characters

Arsène Lupin (a.k.a. His Royal Highness Prince Mirand)
Sherlock Holmes
Frederick, a.k.a. "Little Sherlock," his son
Chief Inspector Ganimard of the Sûreté
Toto Fouinard (Arsène Lupin's assistant)
Miss Maud Clark
Solomon Gottlieb
Rebecca Gottlieb, his sister
Nazir Pasha
Miss Moore
M. Roseroy
M. Lormelles
Madame des Epouffettes
M. Saint-Gatien
Joseph (Gottlieb's servant)
Sergeant Folenfant
Sergeant Dieuzy
Several Other Policemen
A Conductor at the Caen Buffet
A Waiter at the Caen Buffet
A Cashier at the Caen Buffet
Several Travelers at the Caen Buffet
A Newspaper Salesman at the Caen Buffet
Ganimard's Secretary at the Sûreté
An Office Boy at the Sûreté
An Employee of Luna Park
Several Party-Goers (Men and Women)
Baptiste (Prince Mirand's Servant)

A Traffic Policeman
A Cab Driver
Guests at the Hunt (Men and Women)
M. Monnier
A Circus Rider
A Female Clown
The Stationmaster of the Gare du Nord
The Minister

First performed on October 10, 1910, at the Theâtre du Châtelet in Paris, where it played until the end of March, 1911, with M. Julien in the role of Arsène Lupin and M. Houry in the role of Sherlock Holmes.

Act I

Scene I
The Pré-Catalan

The stage represents a tea party at the Pré-Catalan of the Bois de Boulogne during a summer afternoon. In the rear, behind a line of trees, a restaurant pavilion can be seen. In the foreground, tables are placed right and left.

AT RISE, Parisians of all sexes chattering in groups under little tents or around tables. Others arrive or leave by horse or auto or in carriages.

MISS MOORE
Hello, my friends.

ALL
Hello, Miss.

ROSEROY
(to Miss Moore who sits among them)
What, dear friend, you dare to parade around with a necklace like that?

LORMELLES
That's the utmost of imprudence.

MISS MOORE
Why's that?

ROSEROY
Why, because it is splendid and might very well tempt the cupidity of Arsène Lupin!

SAINT-GATIEN
(gaily)
Arsène Lupin! Ah, I'm waiting for that one. You can
no longer find yourself in company these days for
five minutes without the fatality arising of mention-
ing Arsène Lupin. Last year it was Chauterient! This
year it's Arsène Lupin!

LORMELLES
Why, what do you want us of speak of, my dear
chap? A week doesn't pass without the Gentleman
Burglar–for he prides himself on being a gentleman–
accomplishing some new exploit.

ROSEROY
Still, they've set Ganimard on his tracks! Ganimard–
the cleverest detective in the Sûreté.

LORMELLES
That's what he says! But, meanwhile Arsène Lupin
has the laugh on him and slips through his fingers
like a needle!

During this period, Madame des Epouffettes arrives and excitedly approaches the group.

MME. DES EPOUFFETTES
Ah! My friends, how happy I am to meet you. Quick!
Quick! I want details.

ROSEROY
About what?

MME. DES EPOUFFETTES
Why, on the new exploit performed by Arsène Lupin
yesterday at the private picture exhibition at
L'Epatant. Don't you know about it?

ALL

Why, no! No!

SAINT-GATIEN

Arsène Lupin! Not again! Oh no!

At this moment, Prince Mirand appears in the back on horse-back and a young groom, Fouinard, hurries after him.

LORMELLES

(pointing towards the Prince)

Ah! Here's Prince Mirand!

MME. DES EPOUFFETTES

He was certainly at *L'Epatant* and is going to be able to give us information.

MISS MOORE

(with admiration)

Do you think he's still attractive despite his 50 years?

MME. DES EPOUFFETTES

He's marvelous.

MISS MOORE

Yes.

MME. DES EPOUFFETTES

He's truly the King of Elegance!

Mirand has dismounted.

FOUINARD

When will His Highness remount?

MIRAND

In a quarter of an hour.

FOUINARD

Fine, Your Highness!

The groom leads the horse away. Prince Mirand comes forward.

ROSEROY

Come, Prince, come quickly! There's someone here who desires to interview you.

MIRAND

A pretty woman, I hope.

LORMELLES

By Jove–

MME. DES EPOUFFETTES

It's me, my dear Prince.

MIRAND
(kissing her hand)
Oh, then, it's Venus herself!

MME. DES EPOUFFETTES

Tell me, Prince, were you at the private exhibition yesterday at *L'Epatant*?

MIRAND

Naturally.

MME. DES EPOUFFETTES

Then, you must have some details about Arsène Lupin's latest theft?

MIRAND

All the details! And I can swear to you it exceeds in
the unexpected and in comedy all those accomplished
up to now!

ALL

(curious)
Oh, hurry then, hurry! Tell us!

MIRAND

Well, here, ladies! It was a little after 3 p.m. in the
afternoon. In the great hall, everyone was jostling
in order to admire the superb portrait of Miss Welt,
the American millionairess, by Boldini. Suddenly, in
an adjoining salon, screams were heard. Everyone
rushed! It was an old woman having a nervous
breakdown. They took her away and when they returned to admire the sensational portrait, it had been
removed–and replaced by what? A thousand to one
you cannot guess? By the portrait of the very Inspector of the Sûreté who's been hunting after Lupin
without being able to catch him–by the portrait of
Ganimard himself!
            (everyone begins to laugh)
And, do you know what was written in the corner of
the canvas?

ALL

No.

MIRAND

"*To Ganimard–from his great admirer–Arsène Lupin.*"

Renewed laughter.

13

ROSEROY
What audacity all the same!

MISS MOORE
It's stupefying!

MIRAND
(admiringly)
Ah, yes. A man who knows how to put so much
audacity and whimsy into a theft is no vulgar thief.
He's a dilettante–almost an artist.

SEVERAL VOICES
(protesting)
Oh, Prince!

MIRAND
Why, yes, an artist. Not to mention that each of his
thefts is always accompanied by a little lesson.

SAINT-GATIEN
How's that?

MIRAND
Remember the very day he plundered the Washington
galleries? Didn't he send to Mr. Pelleton a celluloid
comb and a rocking-horse to General Puguart?

LORMELLES
That's–

MIRAND
Ah, believe me, gentlemen, Arsène Lupin is not only
a great artist–he's also a great moralist.

MME. DES EPOUFFETTES

All that's very nice. But, it's quite time to arrest him–
your moralist.

A group of badly-dressed men enter.

MISS MOORE

That's true! There's no longer any security in Paris.
Bah! As for me, it seems I see him everywhere.
(pointing towards the group)
There! Have a look at the people they allow in here!
They look bad enough!

MME. DES EPOUFFETTES

Oh, yes, especially the first one. What a sinister face!
It wouldn't surprise me if he was Arsène Lupin.

MIRAND
(laughing)
Relax, dear friends, that's not Lupin. Quite the oppo-
site, in fact.

SAINT-GATIEN

Who is he then?

MIRAND

Why, that's Ganimard, the Chief Inspector of the
Sûreté.

MISS MOORE

You know him?

MIRAND

Yes. I had to call him when Lupin stole my antique
snuff boxes. You remember?

SAINT-GATIEN

Oh, perfectly.

MIRAND
(to Ganimard)

Good afternoon, Chief Inspector.

GANIMARD

Hush!

MIRAND

What's wrong?

GANIMARD
(low to Mirand)

Hush. I'm coming here to arrest Arsène Lupin.

MIRAND

Ah! Bah!
(lower)
Then Lupin's around here?

GANIMARD

Yes.

MIRAND

How do you know it?

GANIMARD
(pulling a letter from his pocket)

Because he wrote me.

MIRAND

That's not possible.

GANIMARD

Yes. He had the nerve to warn me that he would be coming this morning to Pré-Catalan! Just to spare me the cerebral effort! Don't you think he has some nerve?

MIRAND

Ah! Nerve's not what he lacks. Oh, mercy, my dear Ganimard, rid us of that scoundrel!

GANIMARD

If you think it's easy–he changes his appearance like a handkerchief. One day, he's young, the next, he's old. One day, he's fat, the next, he's thin. As for disguises, let's not mention them. He's Houdini.

MIRAND

Evidently, under these circumstances, it won't be easy for you to catch him.

GANIMARD

Do you know to whom you are speaking, Prince? Oh, but begging your pardon–it's 3 p.m., and that's the hour he told me he would be here. I have to station my men around here.

MIRAND

Go, my dear Ganimard, and good luck.

GANIMARD

Oh, just let him give me one real clue. The place where he will be and the time I can find him–and you will see if I miss him.

Ganimard signals his men and leaves at the same time Gottlieb and Rebecca appear in a carriage.

MME. DES EPOUFFETTES

Oh, there! There's Solomon Gottlieb accompanied by
his sister Rebecca. Let's get out of here quickly. I
don't hold with greeting these *parvenus*.

MIRAND
(astonished)

Why, it seems to me, Ladies, that you often went to
the Gottliebs.

MME. DES EPOUFFETTES

Oh–only to their *soirées*.

MISS MOORE

Everybody goes there. It's a real marketplace! But
outside that, never in life!

LORMELLES

The fact is, it would be a bit much if one had to
kowtow to Gottlieb, simply because he earned some
millions in his jewelry shop.

SAINT-GATIEN

And many more practicing usury.

MIRAND
(protesting)

Come on. A usurer? Him!

LORMELLES

So little that he extorted money from me, the old
crocodile!

MIRAND

Come on. You exaggerate, my dear fellow.

SAINT-GATIEN

Ah, Prince, you aren't going to take up the defense of that vulgar fellow?

MIRAND

Indeed, I will. I've known Gottlieb a long time. I take him to be a very fine may–and think nothing of compromising myself by saying hello to him.

ALL

Oh! Prince!

Everybody lifts their arms to Heaven and leaves while Gottlieb and his sister, wearing an enormous wig, have gotten out of their carriage, bowing to right and left–but no one returns or responds to their greetings. So they go to sit at a table. Mirand goes to them.

MIRAND

Hello, my dear Gottlieb.
(bowing)
Mademoiselle.
(to Gottlieb)
How are you this morning?

GOTTLIEB

(radiant)
Not very bad, Prince, I thank you. Will you do us the honor of sitting with us?

MIRAND

Why, certainly.

GOTTLIEB

And you will really agree to take something? A port, a Madeira, a snifter? Waiter, bring all the bottles.

MIRAND

Ah, I beg you–

GOTTLIEB

Yes, yes. As for me, I never consider the expense. Go on, waiter, go on.

A short pause. Rebecca utters a long sigh.

MIRAND

What's wrong, Mademoiselle Rebecca? Now those were big sighs.

REBECCA

Oh, Prince! I feel so weak, so overwhelmed.

MIRAND

Why, it's true! You are very pale.
(to Gottlieb)
Look, Gottlieb, what are you thinking of? You've got to marry this dear child.

GOTTLIEB

As for me, I ask nothing better–only I can't find anyone willing to marry her.

REBECCA

(vexed)
What do you mean, no one? There've been more than 50 who have asked for my hand.

GOTTLIEB

Fifty! At least three! A professor of boxing, a pedicurist, a Spaniard! As if I wanted to have nephews in Spain.

REBECCA

(furious)

Oh, I know quite well you are refusing everybody; it's because you want me to marry a noble! The gentleman wants to be received in the Faubourg Saint-Germain!

GOTTLIEB

Well, yes, as to that! When one begins by selling nuts and arrives, solely through hard labor and skills to the possession of millions—one owes it to oneself to become a Baron.

MIRAND

Right.

GOTTLIEB

Unfortunately, up to this day, all my efforts have been in vain. And God knows how I have tried to get myself accepted by the Faubourg. Heavens, I even offered to loan a Marquis in a difficult situation money at only 20% interest...

MIRAND

And then—

GOTTLIEB

And then he took my money and kicked me out the door. In the end, Prince, what must one do to be accepted in your set?

MIRAND

Very little, my dear fellow. Quite simply, be a part of it.

GOTTLIEB

Meaning that, as for me, I will never be a part of it.

MIRAND

Who knows?

GOTTLIEB
(very moved)
What do you mean, Prince? Would you have a way
of getting me into the nobility?

MIRAND
I don't say no. You are so sympathetic to me.

GOTTLIEB
Oh, speak! Speak quickly, I implore you.

MIRAND
Here is my idea. Recently, a noble foreigner, Nazir
Pasha, has arrived in Paris. I've had the opportunity
to make his acquaintance. He told me he was sent
here on a special mission by his government. Mesopotamia is, it seems, very hard up at the moment, and
to fill its treasury, has decided to sell one of the most
handsome diamonds of the crown–"The Sultan"–
whose value is worth 30 millions.

GOTTLIEB
Thirty millions. That's a lot!

MIRAND
This operation must remain secret so as not to com-
promise the credit of Mesopotamia. This Nazir Pasha
wants to find a person of confidence in your profes-
sion to discreetly negotiate the sale. And naturally, in
gratitude for services rendered, he would grant the
intermediary whatever he desired. Money, decora-
tions. Truly, even a title of nobility.

GOTTLIEB

A title of nobility! Mine! Why then, Prince, I could
march on an equal footing with the La Rochefou-
caulds and the Montmorencys.

MIRAND

(ironically)

At least!

REBECCA

And, as for me, I could marry some little bepowdered
Marquis.

MIRAND

That's certain!

GOTTLIEB

Ah, my God! Thank you! It's wonderful!

REBECCA

Wonderful!

GOTTLIEB

(suddenly downcast)

Ah, yes, but unfortunately I don't know Nazir Pasha
and, perhaps, he won't accept me as a go-between.

MIRAND

Why, yes. I already had a couple of words with him
yesterday and he's supposed to come here this afternoon so we can speak about it again. I will profit by
the opportunity to present you to him.

GOTTLIEB

(enthusiastically)

Oh! Prince! Prince! Never, no never, will you know
the full extent of my gratitude.

MIRAND
(laughing)
That way, if it doesn't go far, I won't be
disillusioned!

At this moment, Nazir Pasha appears at the back of the stage,
which is crowded. He is following a woman whose rear end he
tries to pinch and who gives him a resounding slap.

MIRAND
(laughing)
Here is Nazir Pasha.
(to Gottlieb)
He's even had himself announced.

Mirand goes to Nazir Pasha.

MIRAND
Hello, dear friend. Feeling well this morning?

NAZIR
(rubbing his cheek)
Warmly.

MIRAND
Come, so I can present Monsieur Solomon Gottlieb
to you–whom I spoke about yesterday–and his sister,
Mademoiselle Rebecca.

NAZIR
(excitedly)
Rebecca? Does she have pretty hair! Ah, hair is
everything in a woman, everything.

MIRAND
Hers is admirable!

NAZIR

Oh, then, quick! Quick!

Mirand leads him to Gottlieb and Rebecca.

MIRAND

My dear Pasha, my friend Monsieur Gottlieb.

GOTTLIEB

(bowing)

Highness!

MIRAND

And Mademoiselle Rebecca Gottlieb, his sister.

REBECCA

(curtsies)

Pasha!

Nazir utters a cry and revolves on his heels.

NAZIR

Ah!

MIRAND

What is it?

NAZIR

Allah be praised! This woman is the Lily of the Valley, the Pearl of the Orient!

GOTTLIEB

Huh?

NAZIR

The chaste blonde fiancée with wavy hair that I've
seen pass by so often in my dreams.

REBECCA
(aside, ravished)
Ah! He is charming!

NAZIR

Ah, Rebecca! Daughter of Dalila and Absalom–how
beautiful you are.

REBECCA
Ah, Pasha, you make me blush.

NAZIR
Ah! What pretty hair you have.

REBECCA
You think so?

NAZIR
(lyrical)
And what marvelous color! Their tawny reflections
recall those of old boilers.

REBECCA
Oh! How poetic you are!

GOTTLIEB
(aside)
Well, he's not run of the mill, this here Pasha.

NAZIR
But I have to leave you.

REBECCA

What, already?

NAZIR

Yes. I have a rendezvous with a diplomat at the skating rink. But I want to see you again–to see you again as soon as possible. Where? Tell me where.

GOTTLIEB

Excellence, if you would really do me the honor of being present at the masked ball I am giving in my magnificent hotel on the Avenue Iena.

NAZIR

Oh! Yes, I accept your ball! I accept it because I am all excited.

REBECCA

Ah, my Pasha! My Pasha!

NAZIR

Till tomorrow, my idol! Till tomorrow, my comet with a long tail.

Nazir moves away.

REBECCA

Oh, his comet. He called me his comet. Ah. Solomon, I am completely moved. It seems to me I'm really on the verge of loving him.

They leave, escorted a few steps by Mirand.

At this moment, shouts are heard: "Stop thief! Thief!" Great uproar. Everyone rises and looks to the right. Those at the left stand on chairs.

Prince Mirand returns, uttering a single word: "Fouinard!"

MIRAND
(shouting)
Oh, down there. Down there, look!

Mirand points. Everyone looks in the direction indicated which allows Fouinard to enter through a thicket, almost out of breath, without being seen. The Prince runs quickly to him.

FOUINARD
The cops have seen me! They're on my heels. I'm lost!

MIRAND
Come on. Quick! Pass everything to me.

FOUINARD
Here, boss.

Fouinard passes Mirand a gold vanity bag and a necklace. The Prince puts it in his pocket. Then he turns and moves away.

At this moment, Ganimard leaps from the thicket and nails Fouinard.

GANIMARD
Ah! This time, I've got you.

Two policemen, dressed as city folk, also seize Fouinard. Everyone rushes in. More uproar.

ALL
(shouting at the same time)
What? What's this? What's the matter?

GANIMARD
(to Fouinard)

Ah, my little Lupin. It's been six months. People have been laughing at Ganimard. But this time it's over.

FOUINARD
(struggling)

I'm not Arsène Lupin! Let me go! I didn't steal anything.

GANIMARD

Ah! You didn't steal anything? We're going to see about that…
(to his men)
Search him.

The policemen search Fouinard. And search.

GANIMARD

Well?

POLICEMAN

Nothing, Chief Inspector.

SECOND POLICEMAN

Nothing.

GANIMARD

Ah! This is too much! Yet I didn't lose sight of him except a second–the time it took him to cross the thicket. See if he threw something in there.

Sergeant Folenfant goes to see.

Mirand comes out of the crowd.

MIRAND

What's wrong?

GANIMARD

What's wrong, Prince? I've just arrested Arsène
Lupin.

MIRAND
(laughing)
Arsène Lupin? This boy! Ah, that's comic! Why, this
is Fouinard, my little groom.

GANIMARD

Your groom? Not possible.

MIRAND

Indeed so! I send him every morning to hold my
horse. Besides, everybody knows him here. The
huntsmen, the waiters.

ALL

Why, yes. It's Fouinard.

MIRAND

You see!

FOLENFANT
(returning)
Chief Inspector, we haven't found a thing.

GANIMARD
(shaken)
Ah, indeed. Could I be mistaken?

MIRAND

Don't doubt it. This boy is a good servant–and I answer for his honesty as for my own.

GANIMARD

Ah! Then, release him.
(furious)
Ah! Damn it all! I ask myself, this damn Lupin, will I
ever catch him?

MIRAND

My word, I ask myself that, too.

GANIMARD

(to his men)
Well, what are you waiting for, blockheads? Are you,
indeed, going to run after him? Damned oafs. What a
sorry piece of luck!

They all leave running.

MIRAND

Fouinard–

FOUINARD

(aside)
Am I going to get it!

MIRAND

–the first time you set to work without my orders I
will kick you out.

Mirand goes to rejoin the ladies as Fouinard bows.

CURTAIN

Scene II

Solomon Gottlieb's dressing room

Solomon Gottlieb is in a dressing gown and Marius is fixing his hair. A rooster costume is placed on the table.

GOTTLIEB
Well, Marius, are you going to keep working on my head much longer?

MARIUS
Five minutes, Monsieur–and not provincial minutes, Paris minutes. Just long enough to put a little gum on your face like this...
> (he takes a pinch from a flask and daubs him)
And to fix some feathers to the right and the left.
> (gums on feathers at random)
Like that–and that will be all.

GOTTLIEB
Ah! It's a charming idea, isn't it, to pick this rooster costume for my masked ball?

MARIUS
Excellent–and especially, very original.

GOTTLIEB
In a few moments, all Paris will be crushed into my salons.

MARIUS
There will be a lot of *chic* people.

GOTTLIEB

I believe you. Prince Mirand himself has formerly promised to come.

MARIUS

What luck! Then, this will be stunning!

There is a knock at the door.

GOTTLIEB

Come in!

Joseph, another servant, enters with a letter on a plate.

GOTTLIEB

What's this, Joseph?

JOSEPH

It's a letter that was just brought for you, Monsieur.

GOTTLIEB

Ah! I bet it's another request for an invitation to my ball. And I've already refused over 2,000!

Joseph retires. Gottlieb reads the letter attentively, then utters a cry.

GOTTLIEB

Oh!

MARIUS

What's the matter, Monsieur?

GOTTLIEB

What's the matter? Listen: "*Monsieur, I inform you that tonight Arsène Lupin will steal the Sultan*

GOTTLIEB (cont'd)
Diamond from the home of Nazir Pasha." And it's
signed: "*An accomplice of Lupin who's been cheated
by him and who is avenging himself.*"

MARIUS
(feigning astonishment)
Oh, for goodness' sake!

GOTTLIEB
This is horrible! It's appalling! If they steal the diamond from Nazir, I am ruined!

MARIUS
Why? I don't understand, Monsieur.

GOTTLIEB
It's quite simple. In exchange for my assistance,
Nazir Pasha has promised me the title of Prince–and
a commission as admiral.

MARIUS
Wow! But, it seems to me that, from the moment you
are warned it's not difficult to parry the blow.

GOTTLIEB
How? How?

MARIUS
Telephone Nazir Pasha right away to warn him.

GOTTLIEB
Excellent idea.

MARIUS
When one is from Marseilles, one has only ideas like
that.

Gottlieb grabs the telephone.

GOTTLIEB
Hello! Hello! Mademoiselle, I beg you give me
Number 446-24 immediately. It's an emergency.
(to Marius)
This way I'll have a communication right away.

MARIUS
Very–

GOTTLIEB
Hello. Is Nazir Pasha there? Ah, it's you, dear friend.
It's me, Gottlieb. Listen, this is awful. I've just received a letter advising me that tonight Arsène Lupin
intends to steal the Sultan Diamond… Huh? Why,
no, it's not a put-on… What? What should be done?
I don't know… Hide it in your mattress.

MARIUS
Oh, that's too dangerous. Arsène Lupin will find it.
He always finds it–the trickster.

GOTTLIEB
(to Marius)
It's true, that animal is tricky.
(to Nazir)
Well, do you have an idea? No? That doesn't
astonish me.

MARIUS
I've got an idea.

GOTTLIEB
Let's have it quick.
(to Nazir)
Wait, an idea just came to me.

GOTTLIEB (cont'd)
(to Marius)
What is it?

MARIUS

Let Nazir Pasha bring the diamond with him when he comes to the soirée.

GOTTLIEB

Excellent! Excellent!
(to Nazir)
Bring the diamond with you and deliver it to me. Agreed, right? Good!
(he's about to hang up the phone)
And so there will be no error, I will be dressed as a rooster. Till later, dear friend.
(hanging up)
Whew! I can hardly breathe.
(to Marius)
Ah, Marius, you really had a clever idea.

MARIUS

An idea from Marseilles. That says it all.

Marius continues to dress Gottlieb's hair. There is another knock on the door.

GOTTLIEB

Come in.

Joseph enters.

JOSEPH

Monsieur, it's the costumer who's come to dress you.

GOTTLIEB

Let him come in.

Joseph lets the costumer in and leaves.

> GOTTLIEB
>
> Why, it's almost 10:30!

> MARIUS
>
> Another minute and I'm done.

> GOTTLIEB
>
> Hurry!

Marius puts a vaporizer under his nose.

> GOTTLIEB
>
> What's that? Strange odor!

> MARIUS
>
> The vapor of Secottine. It's to blend the feathers of
> the costume with the feathers on your cheek.

> GOTTLIEB
>
> Ah, right.

> MARIUS
>
> It's sufficient for a few seconds of this vapor to
> instantly–
> >> (looking closely at Gottlieb)
> –to instantly close one's eyes and go to sleep.

Gottlieb falls.

> MARIUS
>
> That's it!

The "costumer" locks the door, then removes his disguise,
revealing himself to be–Arsène Lupin.

LUPIN
Monsieur Gottlieb, may I have the honor of intro-
ducing myself: Arsène Lupin, renowned Gentleman
Burglar...

Marius removes his disguise–it is Fouinard.

LUPIN
...And Toto Fouinard, his faithful Lieutenant.

They bow ironically to the unconscious Gottlieb.

FOUINARD
Say, boss, where are we going to stash him?

Lupin opens the cupboard.

LUPIN
There, in the cupboard.

FOUINARD
Perfect!

They pick him up and place him in the cupboard.

FOUINARD
All aboard for Cupboard-by-the-Sea!
(imitating the whistling of a train)
There! That's it. Already arrived at his destination!

They then lock the cupboard.

LUPIN
And now, to work.

Lupin disrobes and Fouinard helps him to assume the rooster
costume.

FOUINARD

(admiringly)

Ah! All there is to say, boss, is what fine work
this is.

LUPIN

(satisfied)

Yes, it's not too bad!

FOUINARD

Not too bad! Say, instead it's stunning. Yesterday
morning you lured Gottlieb into the business and this
very night this dumb Nazir is going to deliver the
diamond to you. Well, really, you could say that's not
slow work.

(with conviction)

Ah, hold on, boss. Since Napoleon, France hasn't had
even one dodger with your power.

LUPIN

(continuing to dress)

It's possible!

FOUINARD

(still helping to dress him)

It's certain. First off, a man who knows how to invent
the character Prince Mirand is surely a man of genius.

LUPIN

Ah, as to that, I admit it. It was well-conceived, indeed. Today, Prince Mirand is the King of Fashion,
the organizer of all parties! The model of all snobs,
the idol of all women. Prince Mirand is the sum of all
that is Paris *chic*.

FOUINARD
(now finished)
There! That's the thing.
(giving Lupin a mirror)
Here, what do you say about it?

LUPIN
Gentry himself.

FOUINARD
Immense! Immense! Then, you're satisfied, boss?

LUPIN
Enchanted, my boy.

FOUINARD
So much the better because I have something to ask
of you.

LUPIN
Ask.

FOUINARD
Will you permit me to take away the telephone?

LUPIN
Why?

FOUINARD
It will look so well on my desk.

He tries to take it off.

LUPIN
Will you leave that alone?

FOUINARD

But–

LUPIN

Will you leave it alone! Go! Reopen the door right
away.

FOUINARD
(vexed)
Ah, indeed. This is disgusting. You are going to take
an enormous diamond worth 30 millions–and as for
me, I can't even carry off a wretched telephone worth
32 francs and one-half.

Fouinard goes to open the door.

LUPIN

That's enough.

A knock on the door.

LUPIN

Just in time! Come in.

Joseph enters.

LUPIN
(in Gottlieb's voice)
What's wrong?

JOSEPH

There's an ill-dressed man who insists on seeing you
right away.

LUPIN
Ah! He gave you his name?

JOSEPH

He told me to announce Chief Inspector Ganimard.

FOUINARD
(aside, trembling)
Uh-oh.

LUPIN
(low to Fouinard)
Get hold of yourself.
(aloud)
Why, have him come in right away!

Joseph leaves. Fouinard gets on all fours and tries to hide under the toilet. Lupin catches him.

LUPIN
Will you stay here, animal!

FOUINARD
Oh! Mama! Mama!

Ganimard enters and is rather astonished to see the man whom he believes to be Gottlieb dressed up in a rooster costume.

GANIMARD
Is that you, Monsieur Gottlieb?

LUPIN
Yes, Monsieur, it is I, Gottlieb.

GANIMARD
Impossible to tell under that disguise. I am Chief Inspector Ganimard of the Sûreté. You've heard of me, I think?

LUPIN

Have I heard of you? Why, at this moment, all of
Paris has its eyes fixed upon you.

GANIMARD

I know it; I know it.

LUPIN

May I know what brings you?

GANIMARD

Something serious, very serious. Nazir Pasha just
telephoned me on the subject of the letter written to
you by an accomplice of Arsène Lupin. Will you
show it to me?

LUPIN

(to Fouinard)
Why, yes. My boy, will you give the Chief Inspector
the letter?

Fouinard hands Ganimard the letter.

GANIMARD

Ah! Hum. Ho-ho!

LUPIN

What do you think of it?

GANIMARD

Nothing at the moment–but on reflection–after a
while–

LUPIN

Why, take an hour–two hours if you like. Here's an
excellent armchair. Install yourself.

GANIMARD
(sitting)
Thanks.

Ganimard takes his head in his hands as he looks at the letter and ponders.

Rebecca appears. She's dressed as Little Bo-Peep, a costume that is much too young for her age and looks somewhat ridiculous on her. The hair of her wig falls very low and are ruffled.

REBECCA
Well, Solomon, are you ready? Our guests are beginning to arrive.
(fidgeting)
How do you like me in this costume?

LUPIN
(trying to keep a straight face)
Delicious.

REBECCA
Isn't it? I think my hair will please him this way.

LUPIN
Ah, indeed! Surely. How he's going to be flabbergasted.

REBECCA
(simpering)
Only, it seems to me that I look... perhaps a trifle too young in this.

LUPIN
(forcing himself not to guffaw)
No, not at all, indeed!

REBECCA

Yes, yes. I feel like 15.

LUPIN

At a minimum.

REBECCA

I hope that Nazir doesn't find me too young to pay
me court now.

LUPIN

No, don't worry. It won't come to that. Come on. Go
quickly. I will join you.

REBECCA

Eight. I look eight years old.

Rebecca leaves as Lupin guffaws stealthily.

LUPIN

(to Fouinard)
Go close the door.

Fouinard packs up the outfit used by Marius and goes to close
the door as Lupin returns to Ganimard.

LUPIN

My dear Monsieur Ganimard, excuse me for leaving
you but my guests reclaim me.

GANIMARD

(still absorbed in his thoughts)
Go! Go! As for me, I am working.

LUPIN

Believe me, don't force your ideas too much. It's very bad for the brain.
> (to Fouinard)

Come, my boy.

Lupin leaves. Fouinard remains behind and grasps the telephone.

FOUINARD

I knew I would have it!

Fouinard leaves, locking the door behind him.

GANIMARD

> (alone)

Is this a trick or not? That's the whole of it. If I go to Nazir's party and I manage to catch Lupin, it's a triumph–but if I wait for him there and he doesn't show up–it's a blunder. What to do? Ah! Bah! I'm going to go. Only, I will go there in disguise! That way, no one will know that I'm there–

Ganimard goes to the door and finds it locked; he shakes it as he tries to open it, but in vain.

GANIMARD

Locked. Why did they lock the door? That's stupid.

He tries the door on the right, but it's locked too.

GANIMARD

Locked also. Ah, indeed, that's too much. Open up, open up, will you?

At this moment, a paper is slipped under the door. Ganimard takes it and cautiously unfolds it.

GANIMARD

A note? It's from Arsène Lupin! "*Dear Friend, they
will let you out after Nazir Pasha has delivered the
diamond to me. Arsène Lupin.*" What does this mean?
Oh, my head–my head!

Suddenly, he hears groaning coming from the cupboard.

GANIMARD

Huh? What's that? Groaning? Is there someone
in there?
(pulling a huge revolver)
Ah, we'll see who has the last laugh!

He goes to the door and opens it.

GANIMARD

Come out, my good man!

Gottlieb comes out, red as a tomato, choking. He sees the revolver pointed at him and recoils, terrified.

GOTTLIEB

Mercy! Pity! Don't kill me. I'm Gottlieb.

GANIMARD

That's not true! You're Arsène Lupin!

GOTTLIEB

No indeed! No indeed! I swear to you that I am Gottlieb. The real–the only Gottlieb.

GANIMARD

(agitated)
Why, then–if you are the real Gottlieb, who is it that
just left and received me in your place dressed like a
rooster?

GOTTLIEB

Like a rooster? I get it!

GANIMARD

What? What? What is it you're getting? If you
understand anything, say it, because, as for me,
I don't understand a thing.

GOTTLIEB

The hairdresser wasn't a real hairdresser.

GANIMARD

Ah! Really. Well, if the hairdresser wasn't a real
hairdresser, who then was the hairdresser?

GOTTLIEB

Why, Arsène Lupin of course, for God's sake!

GANIMARD

Arsène Lupin?

GOTTLIEB

Why, yes! It was he who put me to sleep with the
chloroform and locked me in this cupboard.

GANIMARD

Ah! You think so?

GOTTLIEB

And while we're both here, he is at the ball in my
place–and it's he who is going to receive the Sultan
Diamond from the hands of Nazir Pasha!

GANIMARD
(striking his head)
Heavens! Why, it's true, in fact! He just wrote me so.

GOTTLIEB

We must prevent that–prevent it at all costs. Come,
quick, quick!

GANIMARD

There's only one problem. There's no way to leave.
Lupin has locked all the doors. He has had the nerve
to imprison me, Ganimard, Chief Inspector of the
Sûreté!

GOTTLIEB

Since you are the famous police detective, you
must have a plan–an idea.

GANIMARD

Yes. We'll wait until someone comes to let us out.

He sits down.

GOTTLIEB

Why, this is abominable! To know you're going to be
robbed and to be unable to do anything! Nothing!
(letting out a shout)
Ah! Yes–

GANIMARD

What?

GOTTLIEB

I'm going to telephone for my men to come and release us. Ah! The bandit has taken the phone–and
only left the cord. Ah, My God! How to get out of
here?
(uttering another cry)
Ah!

GANIMARD
What? Again? It's idiotic to cause frights like that.

Gottlieb points to the fireplace.

GOTTLIEB
There it is! The exit. There it is.

GANIMARD
The fireplace?

GOTTLIEB
Yes. Let's hurry. You go first.

GANIMARD
But we're going to be filthy after we get out of there.

GOTTLIEB
True, but the chimney will be swept for the winter
and that will save me some money.

CURTAIN

Scene III

The Costume Ball at Gottlieb's

The ballroom of Gottlieb's mansion is luxuriously decorated with flowers and velours hangings fringed with gold. Electric lights flood the hall with light. Guests everywhere mill about in diverse costumes. At the back, there is a grand staircase with a double set of steps. Much excitement is occurring when curtain rises.

Lupin appears, in his rooster costume. He acts agitated.

LUPIN
(aside)
Oh–and this Nazir who hasn't arrived yet! I'm really impatient!

Rebecca enters.

REBECCA
Ah, my brother, if you knew the success that I'm having. Everybody finds me ravishing in this costume. Oh, I wish indeed that my dear Pasha were here!

LUPIN
Me, too.

REBECCA
Oh, he won't be late–love has ways.

Just at that moment, Nazir finally enters, rather grotesquely dressed as Cupid.

REBECCA

Heavens! What was I saying—there he is! And with
wings.

She rushes to Nazir.

REBECCA

Oh, sweet friend, it's you at last!

NAZIR

Star of the Orient, comet with a luminous tail...

REBECCA
(simpering)
Oh! Be quiet. You're making me blush.

NAZIR

Ah, what a delicious costume. And what hair!

Lupin approaches them.

LUPIN
(in Gottlieb's voice)
Excuse me for interrupting you. The diamond.

NAZIR

That's fair. Love has made me forget everything.
(to Rebecca)
Two minutes, adorable Sultana, two little minutes
and I'm yours.

REBECCA

I don't know if I ought to grant them.

LUPIN
(low to Rebecca)
Beat it. And fast!

REBECCA
(vexed and surprised)
Oh!

She steps aside.

LUPIN
Now, quickly, the diamond.

Nazir searches in his pocket and gives the stone to Lupin.

NAZIR
Here it is! Whew! I have one less weight on my stomach.

Lupin pockets it.

LUPIN
Enchanted to have relieved you. But, here's the Ballet from the Opera. I'm going to take this opportunity to put the diamond in my safe. Go, quickly, rejoin my darling little sister!

NAZIR
I fly! I fly!

Nazir makes his Cupid wings flap and goes off.

LUPIN
(aside)
And, as for me, I'm flying off.

Lupin leaves. There is a ballet interlude.

Then, Gottlieb and Ganimard enter in a gust of wind. They are covered with soot.

GOTTLIEB/GANIMARD
Stop him! Stop him!

They are out of breath. All the guests laugh uproariously when they see them and surround them.

REBECCA
What funny costumes.

NAZIR
Merciful Allah! It's Gottlieb. So, you've changed costumes?

GOTTLIEB
(turning pale)
Me? You've seen me in another costume?

NAZIR
Just now you were a rooster...
(low)
...When I gave you the diamond.

GOTTLIEB
Robbed! I've been robbed!

Gottlieb collapses in Ganimard's arms.

NAZIR
Come on, don't play the fool, because I recognized you.

Nazir leaves, pulling Rebecca.

GANIMARD
(angry at Gottlieb)
It's your fault, too. Why did you make your chimney
so narrow that it takes an hour to climb out?

GOTTLIEB
Why, I could hardly foresee that I would be forced to
leave my own office through the fireplace.

GANIMARD
A banker must foresee every eventuality, Monsieur.

At this moment, Prince Mirand enters, disguised as French
King Charles IX.

MIRAND
Ah, my dear Gottlieb, permit me to congratulate you.
What a splendid party.

GOTTLIEB
Prince.

MIRAND
You know, your chimney-sweep costume is very
funny–a real masterpiece.
(recognizing Ganimard)
Heavens! If I'm not mistaken–it is you, isn't it, Chief
Inspector? And you're also disguised as a chimney
sweep. Why, it's strange. Neither of you seem
amused.

GOTTLIEB
Ah! Prince. What's just happened to me is shocking.
Arsène Lupin–

MIRAND
Him again!

GANIMARD

Always him!

GOTTLIEB

He's stolen the diamond that Nazir Pasha brought with him.

MIRAND

For Heavens' sake!

GOTTLIEB

It's a disaster—more. It's a catastrophe!

GANIMARD

A complete catastrophe.

MIRAND

Come, come, gentlemen! Do not panic and let's focus. First, does Nazir Pasha know of the theft?

GOTTLIEB

No.

MIRAND

Then, nothing is lost. It's only a matter of hiding that fact from him until…

GOTTLIEB

Until I've received my commission as Prince and Admiral.

MIRAND

Yes, and until Lupin is arrested. Which will happen soon, I'm sure. After all, isn't Monsieur Ganimard already here?

GANIMARD

Obviously, I am here. It's Lupin who no longer is.

MIRAND

Bah! You'll meet him soon enough.

GANIMARD

Oh, if he'd only give me a rendezvous somewhere, the rascal.

Joseph approaches Gottlieb with a silver tray.

JOSEPH

They've just brought this urgent letter for Monsieur Ganimard.

GANIMARD

That's me. Police business, no doubt. You'll excuse me, gentlemen.

GOTTLIEB/MIRAND

By all means.

GANIMARD

Ah!

GOTTLIEB/MIRAND

What's wrong?

GANIMARD

It's from Arsène Lupin.

GOTTLIEB

What does he say?

GANIMARD

My dear Ganimard: Always eager to spare you any cerebral effort, I am informing you that I will travel to New York next Saturday on the S.S. Provence, *in order to sell the Sultan Diamond to some American millionaire. Cordially, Arsène Lupin.*

MIRAND

Oh!

GOTTLIEB

Ah! This time, it's the end of everything.

GANIMARD

There it is!

MIRAND

What?

GANIMARD

The imbecile is delivering himself to me.

MIRAND/GOTTLIEB

What do you mean?

GANIMARD

What do I mean? The day after tomorrow, I will be in Le Havre and I will arrest Lupin the moment he sets foot on that ship. That's all, gentlemen, that's all.

MIRAND

Oh, bravo! Bravo! Now, there's an admirable plan!
(aside)
That way, I'll be able to leave from Cherbourg in complete safety.

CURTAIN

Act II

Scene IV
The Buffet at the Railway Station of Caen

The stage represents the Buffet at the Railway Station of Caen in Normandy. At the back, there are three large, open doors through which one can see the station with its trains and passengers coming and going. A station manager gives orders; a conductor answers the questions of an officer; porters push luggage carts; a police officer is on duty. In the Buffet room itself, travelers are eating or being served. Some are seated at a long table in the middle, others at small tables, drinking boiling coffee which they have just served themselves. One sees piles of luggage and other articles of travel.

AT RISE, a train is in the station. At one small table, there is a traveler, a little boy and a dog. All three are seated on chairs.

> ALL THE TRAVELERS
> (calling at the same time)
> Waiter! Look, waiter, this coffee is too hot!
> Undrinkable.

A Conductor enters at the back.

> CONDUCTOR
> Travelers to Meyden, Falaise, Argenton and
> Le Mans–boarding now!

> VARIOUS TRAVELERS
> What? Already! Oh!

Some put their cups to their lips, burn themselves and utter screams.

> WAITER
> (sadistic)
> Don't rush, ladies and gentlemen, don't rush. You still have 15 seconds.

> TRAVELER No. 1
> (furious)
> And no way to drink this coffee! It's insane!

The travelers leave money on the tables. They rush, jostling each other onto the platform.

Traveler No. 1 hands a large banknote to the Waiter.

> TRAVELER No. 1
> Waiter, quick, pay yourself.

> WAITER
> (slowly, on purpose)
> Let's see. You had a café-crème with bread...

> TRAVELER No. 1
> (stamping his foot)
> Yes–my change–my change.

> WAITER
> With bread... and butter, I think...

> CONDUCTOR
> Travelers to Meyden, Falaise, Argenton and Le Mans–boarding now!

TRAVELER No. 1
Yes, yes. Fine! Fine! Keep the change then!

WAITER
(pocketing the money)
It always ends the same way.

Very calmly, he replaces the uneaten food in the buffet.

As he is about to pay the Cashier, a Second Traveler is looking
for his overcoat in his suitcase.

TRAVELER No. 2
Now, that's it. My coat has vanished!

CASHIER
Don't worry, Monsieur. We'll look for it.

TRAVELER No. 2
Look for it, yes. My train is about to leave.
(he offers his card)
Here's my address! You will send it to me. It's a
yellow overcoat. And if you don't find it, I will
demand 1,000 francs in damages from your rotten
company.

He runs out.

CASHIER
(aside)
And they will give you 100 *sous*. You should have
read the tariff.

Another Traveler (TRAVELER No. 3) rises to leave. At that
moment, the traveler with the little boy–who is none other
than Sherlock Holmes–rises and goes to him.

HOLMES

Excuse me, sir! Will you allow me to ask you a question?

TRAVELER No. 3

By all means, Monsieur.

HOLMES

Why are you so hot?

TRAVELER No. 3

(surprised)

What do you say?

HOLMES

I say that you have on nothing but a light Macfarlane and therefore you shouldn't perspire because it's very cool this morning.

TRAVELER No. 3

Why, Monsieur–

HOLMES

So, if you are perspiring, it's because under the Macfarlane, you have another coat–and that this coat is probably the one you've just "borrowed" from this gentleman.

TRAVELER No. 3

Monsieur?

HOLMES

Come on, no scenes! Take it off, I beg you, and go give it back to its rightful owner. And now, I won't keep you any longer. Sir, I have, indeed, the honor–

Traveler No. 3 leaves speechless, obeying Holmes' orders as if he was hypnotized. The Detective sits down tranquilly.

FREDERICK
(with admiration)
Ah! Bravo, Papa. You are truly the greatest detective in the world.

HOLMES
Oh, a simple consulting detective, Frederick.

FREDERICK
Yes, but smarter than all the other detectives combined. Oh, Papa, one day I'd like to be as good a detective as you.

HOLMES
It doesn't suffice to want to! Detectives are born–not made. You can perfect the necessary qualities, but you must first have them within. Do you possess these qualities, Frederick?

FREDERICK
Oh, yes, Papa. Heavens, at school, every time crayons vanish from the desks of one of my friends, I'm always the one who discovers who's stolen them.

HOLMES
Really? And how do you find the culprit?

FREDERICK
Ah! This way. First off, I make a detailed investigation, then I consider the clues, and by deduction, I always find the culprit. I must have a knack for it! Why, I've got almost as much *flair* as Toby here.

He caresses the dog.

HOLMES
In that case, you have a lot.

FREDERICK
Plenty! Oh, Papa, it would be so nice if you were to take me as your student.

HOLMES
I'm not saying I won't, Frederick. Once I've determined that you truly have the necessary qualities.

Holmes pulls out his pipe and fills it. The newspaper salesman enters the Buffet with his basket.

NEWSPAPER SALESMAN
Ask for the Paris papers. New theft by Arsène Lupin.

FREDERICK
Arsène Lupin! Oh, Papa, will you buy the paper? I would like to know what he's done this time, this Lupin. I find this Gentleman Burglar exciting.

HOLMES
You're right, Frederick. That fellow Lupin is an interesting character.
(calling)
Hey! Merchant.

NEWSPAPER SALESMAN
The Caen paper, Monsieur?

HOLMES
No–the Paris paper–*Le Figaro*.

NEWSPAPER SALESMAN
Here!

HOLMES

Thanks!

Holmes pays the newsman who goes off.

FREDERICK

Oh, read, Papa, read.

Holmes unfolds the paper and starts reading.

HOLMES

*We have just learned that, last night, Arsène Lupin
stole a priceless diamond from M. Gottlieb, a re-
spected jeweler. The famous Chief Inspector Ganimard of the Sûreté, having discovered, with his usual
perspicacity, that Lupin was planning to leave for
America, went immediately to Le Havre where he is
certain of arresting him very soon.*
(to Frederick)
Well, Frederick, here's an opportunity to prove your
abilities as a detective. Let's see–tell me what you
think of this business.

FREDERICK

What do I think of it?
(concentrating)
First of all, I am certain of one thing.

HOLMES

Which is?

FREDERICK

That this Ganimard is an imbecile.

HOLMES

Ah, and why?

FREDERICK

Because it's almost as if he had written to Lupin,
"I am going to Le Havre, so don't go there."

HOLMES

Not bad, Frederick. And in your opinion, what's
Lupin going to do?

FREDERICK

Since he must rid himself of the diamond, and it's
only in America where anyone is rich enough to buy
it from him, he'll take either an English or German
liner to get there.

HOLMES

And, as the German line is the most rapid, it is most
probably that he is embarking from Cherbourg!

FREDERICK

That's elementary. Oh, Papa, since we are passing
through Cherbourg to return to England, do you think
that it would be amusing to meet Lupin and make his
acquaintance?

HOLMES

Evidently, Fred! But, it remains to be seen if he will
be disposed to make ours.

At this moment, an automobilist enters with his chauffeur. It's
Arsène Lupin, with his real face, the one we saw when he was
in Gottlieb's dressing room. The chauffeur is Fouinard.

Holmes follows him with his eyes during the following scene.

LUPIN

(furious)

I tell you, it's your fault. An automobile never breaks down if its chauffeur knows his business.

FOUINARD

Boss, I'm truly sorry.

LUPIN

That's fine, that's fine.

(to the waiter)

Tell me, *garçon*, can you tell me how soon there will be a train to Cherbourg?

WAITER

I don't know, Monsieur. I work for the café–I handle the hot coffee.

Lupin exasperated, turns around and notices the Conductor.

LUPIN

Ah, a conductor.

CONDUCTOR

Monsieur?

LUPIN

What time is the train for Cherbourg?

CONDUCTOR

I don't know, Monsieur.

LUPIN

What do you mean, you don't know? Ah, this is insane. No one knows anything in this station. And there's not one sign.

CONDUCTOR
On the West-East, the trains come and go when they
please. That's the general rule.

LUPIN
(bitter)
That's charming.

Fouinard notices a piece of cutlery on the table, takes off his
goggles and puts the cutlery in his pocket.

FOUINARD
Oh, nice cutlery.

LUPIN
I still must take the boat to Cherbourg this very day.

HOLMES
(low to Frederick)
To Cherbourg! Did you hear, Frederick?

FREDERICK
Yes, Papa.

Meanwhile, Lupin has noticed Fouinard's petty theft.

LUPIN
What is that you've got hidden in your pocket again?

FOUINARD
Oh, boss, a no-account piece of cutlery.

Lupin makes an angry, silent gesture at his assistant.

FOUINARD
It's not silver, it's only electroplated.

LUPIN
(exasperated)
It's for that that this idiot–

FOUINARD
What can I do? I can't help myself!

LUPIN
Come on! Leave it.

Fouinard replaces the cutlery.

HOLMES
(low)
Frederick, listen to what I'm going to tell you.

FREDERICK
Yes, Papa.

Holmes whispers in his son's ear. The Newspaper Salesman reappears.

NEWSPAPER SALESMAN
Ask for the Paris papers! Complete details of Arsène Lupin's latest theft.

Fouinard and Lupin, who were about to leave, abruptly reappear.

LUPIN
Huh? Did you hear that?

FOUINARD
Yes! I heard.

NEWSPAPER SALESMAN
The latest exploit of Lupin and his gang!

FOUINARD
His gang. Ah! That's me.

Fouinard sees a policeman pass by on the platform and collapses on a chair.

LUPIN
What's wrong with you?

FOUINARD
It's that policeman passing by. Give me a glass of
water. With some brandy.

Lupin pours him a drink.

LUPIN
Go on, coward.

FOUINARD
I'm not a coward—only, I have cold feet.

LUPIN
Bah! No one knows you here.

FOUINARD
I sincerely hope so.

HOLMES
(low to Frederick)
Agreed, Frederick?

FREDERICK
Agreed, Papa.

Frederick goes off.

> LUPIN
> (to Fouinard who has drunk)
> Come on, get up and try to get hold of yourself.
> People are looking at us.

> FOUINARD

Yes, boss.

> LUPIN
> (very loud)
> Decidedly, my dear fellow, we must go and look for
> the Station Master, since no one knows anything
> here.

Holmes pulls his train schedule from his valise.

> HOLMES

Pardon, sir.

> LUPIN

Monsieur?

> HOLMES
> Would you allow me to loan you my schedule?

> LUPIN
> Very gladly, Monsieur.

Lupin looks at the schedule while Holmes never takes his eyes
from him.

Frederick suddenly appears at the door and shouts:

> FREDERICK
> Hello, Monsieur Lupin!

Lupin and Fouinard turn and look at each other for a moment, caught by surprise, trying to figure out where that shout came from.

HOLMES
(aside)
That's him all right.
(to Lupin, very friendly)
Please forgive my son for that little joke. It was I who ordered him to do it.

LUPIN
(regaining his cool)
A joke? I don't get it.

HOLMES
You will. I must first tell you that I am by nature very observant and I really enjoy studying everything around me.

LUPIN
That's your right, Monsieur.

HOLMES
There was your rapid manner of entering here, your rage against the employees who refused to give you information, your nervousness at your inability to se-cure a train schedule. All that made me think that you were in a great hurry to reach Cherbourg.

LUPIN
Indeed? And so?

HOLMES
You left to look for the Station Master when the Newspaper Salesman started shouting, "*Ask for the*

HOLMES (cont'd)

latest theft by Arsène Lupin." At the same moment, a
police officer passed by the gate and your companion, after having gone pale, almost fell into a faint.

LUPIN

The poor lad! He's so weak, so delicate. Ah, you
have to take good care of him.

FOUINARD

Oh, yes, the best care in the world.

Fouinard begins to cough in a comic way.

HOLMES

Yes, especially when he has cutlery from this Buffet
in his pocket.

FOUINARD
(aside)

Damn!

HOLMES

From all this, the truth became transparent in my
mind. But to be even more certain, I sent my son
Frederick to shout an agreed-upon welcome. Surprise
at being recognized made you blink. Oh, very lightly,
I agree, but enough to allow me to say to you, "My
dear sir, you are Arsène Lupin–the famous Gentleman Burglar."

LUPIN

And you, Monsieur, if I may judge by the accuracy of
your deductions, must be Sherlock Holmes, the notorious consulting detective?

HOLMES
(bowing)
In person.

LUPIN
Delighted, my dear Mister Holmes, to make your acquaintance.

HOLMES
The same goes for me, my dear Monsieur Lupin!

Fouinard, terrified, is hiding under a table.

FOUINARD
We are toast.

LUPIN
Then, Monsieur, I think there remains only one thing for you to do.

HOLMES
What's that?

LUPIN
To have me arrested.

HOLMES
(haughtily)
What do you take me for? If you are a gentleman burglar, as for me, I am a detective, a man of the world. You are in the habit of warning people you are about to rob, aren't you? Well, I insist on warning those I intend to arrest. To each his style.

LUPIN
All my apologies, Mister Holmes. Indeed, I misunderstood you.

HOLMES
Allow me to introduce my son Frederick.

FREDERICK
Bonjour, Monsieur.

LUPIN
Heavens, he speaks French very correctly.

HOLMES
He was raised in France.

LUPIN
Bonjour, my little friend.
(to Holmes)
He's charming.

HOLMES
(more friendly)
While waiting for the arrival of our train, would you
allow me to offer you something?

LUPIN
With pleasure!

HOLMES
Waiter!

WAITER
Here! Here!

FOUINARD
What about me? Aren't you going to invite me?

LUPIN
You! Go check the bags, idiot.

FOUINARD

Right, boss. I'm always the one who pays while
others drink.

HOLMES

What will you have?

LUPIN

A glass of sherry.

HOLMES
(to the waiter)
Two sherrys.

FREDERICK

And for me, an absinthe.

FOUINARD

An absinthe? That kid can get around without his
nurse-maid.

Fouinard passes near a waiter holding a basket with bottles.
He takes one and leaves by the rear.

HOLMES

Then, it would appear, Monsieur Lupin, that you are
leaving for America?

LUPIN

Yes, and I won't hide the fact that it's not without a
certain trepidation that I am returning there.

HOLMES

You've had some difficulties with the police there?

LUPIN

Oh, you know, the police… That's never something to bother me.

The waiter leaves after having served them.

LUPIN

No, it's the memory of a certain adventure.

HOLMES

A love adventure?

LUPIN

Precisely. Two years ago, in New York, I fell in love with a charming young girl, and she wasn't indifferent to me. But, in America, poor suitors aren't welcome, and when I introduced myself to Maud's father to ask for her hand, I was immediately shown the door.

HOLMES

And then what did you do?

LUPIN

What could I do? I returned to France, sad to see my happiness ruined by a miserable question of money. So then, to restore the balance of my finances, I decided to take from the pocket of my fellow men what was lacking in mine. And that is how André Largery became Arsène Lupin.

HOLMES

A fine tale. I understand. Ah! It's truly a shame that you are leaving.

LUPIN

Why?

HOLMES

Because, just now, reading this paper–the thought came to me of busying myself with this Sultan Diamond business.

LUPIN

Really?

HOLMES

I don't need to return to London for four days and I confess that I would have been happy to devote those four days to you.

LUPIN

Oh, I am sorry to disappoint you, but I have to leave.

HOLMES

Your decision is irrevocable?

LUPIN

Irrevocable.

HOLMES

Let's not talk about it, then. To your health!

LUPIN

And to yours!

FREDERICK

To your amours, Monsieur Lupin.

LUPIN
(laughing)
Thanks, young man.

At this moment, we hear the whistle of a train arriving from Paris, on its way to Cherbourg. There is a new eruption of travelers into the Buffet.

TRAVELERS
Waiter! Waiter! Some coffee.

WAITER
Here! Ladies and gentlemen, here!

The waiter rapidly serves the boiling-hot coffee. The travelers try to drink and utter cries of pain.

TRAVELERS
This is undrinkable. It's too hot! Ah! Is this a joke?

As the travelers berate the indifferent waiter, Maud Clark enters the buffet.

MAUD
Waiter, something to write with.

WAITER
Right away, Madame!

Maud sits at a small table behind Arsène Lupin in such a way that only Sherlock Holmes can see her. The waiter brings her writing materials.

CONDUCTOR
Travelers for Lisieux, Bernay, Evreux, Nantes and Paris–all aboard!

TRAVELERS
(furious)
What? Already?

WAITER

Don't rush, ladies and gentlemen. Don't rush. You still have 15 seconds.

TRAVELERS

Fifteen seconds! This is ridiculous. There's no way to drink that coffee!

CONDUCTOR

Travelers for Lisieux, Bernay, Evreux, Nantes and Paris–all aboard!

TRAVELERS

OK! Here–pay yourself. Keep the change. I don't have the time.

The travelers rush back, jostling each other to get to the train.

WAITER

That never fails.

Maud gets up.

MAUD

Waiter! Here's five francs to send this telegram right away.

WAITER

Thank you, Madame.

Maud heads toward the platform. Lupin notices and recognizes her. Unable to repress a gesture, he rises abruptly.

LUPIN
(to Holmes)

I beg your pardon, but I just noticed a friend. You'll excuse me.

HOLMES

Why, of course.

Lupin exits to the platform

The waiter replaces the coffee and snacks in his thermos. Holmes watches Lupin.

WAITER

For the next train.

HOLMES

My! My! It's the lady who was there just now that he's pursuing. She's getting in her compartment...

We hear the whistle of the departing train.

HOLMES

The train is leaving and Lupin remains on the platform, planted like a statue.

Holmes goes to the table at which Maud was sitting.

HOLMES

She wrote a telegram and dried it on the blotter. Perhaps it transferred... Yes!
(reading backward)
"To *Electric Hotel, Paris. Please reserve me a room. Miss Clark.*" That's perfect. Well, what do you think of it, Frederick?

FREDERICK

That this lady could be the one Lupin was telling us about.

HOLMES

Indeed. Excellent, Frederick. I am well pleased with you.

Holmes replaces the blotter on the table and writes the information in a notebook. Lupin returns.

LUPIN

I'm sorry to have left you so abruptly, but it was an old friend.

FREDERICK
(sarcastically)
She's rather well-preserved, your "old friend."

LUPIN
(wistfully)
Yes, she is.

There is a bell ringing outside.

HOLMES

Ah! I think that's the bell that announces our train. It will be here in a few minutes. Let's move to the platform.

LUPIN

It's that—I'm no longer leaving—with you.

HOLMES

Really?

LUPIN

Yes—the friend that I met just now insisted so much that I return to Paris to spend a few days—that I was unable to refuse.

HOLMES

Oh, Monsieur Lupin, it's not kind to lack confidence in me.

LUPIN

What do you mean?

HOLMES

If you are returning to Paris, it's to be with your "old friend," a rather charming lady.

LUPIN
(after a moment)
Decidedly, I see that nothing escapes you.

HOLMES

No big thing. Well, I renew my proposition. I have four days before me. Would you like me to devote them to you?

LUPIN

This is serious? Would you do that?

HOLMES

Nothing could be more serious.

LUPIN

Then, Arsène Lupin versus Sherlock Holmes?

HOLMES

Exactly.

LUPIN

All right!

Holmes pulls out his watch.

HOLMES

You have a chronometer?

Lupin pulls out his own watch.

LUPIN

An excellent one–I got it from Mr. Vanderbilt.

HOLMES

Shall we set our watches together?

LUPIN

Gladly! I have a quarter to twelve.

HOLMES

Today is Monday. By 6 p.m. on Friday, I will have
arrested you and retrieved the Sultan Diamond.

LUPIN
(with a smile)
You may try.

FREDERICK

We will try!

HOLMES

But as I think it is essential that, during these four
days, you are completely at ease, please allow me to
tell you that the lady in question plans to stay at the
Electric Hotel.

LUPIN
(astonished)
How do you know that?

HOLMES

Oh! That's elementary. She telegraphed. So, by looking at the blotter like this–

He shows him the blotter, backward. Lupin looks at it and whistles admiringly.

LUPIN

My compliments! But, as one politeness deserves another, would you allow me to render you a small service in turn?

HOLMES

Which one?

LUPIN

Just this. The privilege of capturing me rightly belongs to the French Police, and I think they would look ill upon an amateur detective, especially a foreign one, meddling in their affairs. You will be poorly received, unless a word of introduction from me to Chief Inspector Ganimard smoothes things for you.

HOLMES

Really? But I'd be afraid of abusing–

LUPIN

Not at all. I'm very happy to oblige.

Lupin scribbles a note on his card as the Paris-Cherbourg Express arrives. He then hands the card to Holmes, who takes it.

LUPIN

With this, all doors will open before you.

HOLMES

My most sincere thanks.

LUPIN

Monsieur Ganimard is in his office every day from
five to six. When I have something to ask of him, it's
always at that time that I go there.

HOLMES

Thank you. On arriving in Paris tomorrow, I will go
directly to see Monsieur Ganimard.

LUPIN
(astonished)
You aren't leaving today?

HOLMES

No, Frederick and I don't know Caen and since we
are here, we might as well profit by the visit, don't
you agree?

LUPIN

Evidently.

The train's departing whistle blows. Fouinard reappears,
looking distracted.

FOUINARD

Boss! Boss! The train just left.

LUPIN

That's no matter! We are returning to Paris.

FOUINARD
(terrified)
To Paris! Ah, that's really dangerous.

LUPIN

(to Holmes)

My train won't be here for another hour! While waiting, my dear Mister Holmes, will you do me the great honor of having lunch with me?

HOLMES

(hesitating)

Why–

LUPIN

Oh, you can't refuse. It will be our last lunch before our duel begins, that's all.

HOLMES

So be it, then!

They sit at a table for lunch.

LUPIN

Waiter!

CURTAIN

Scene V

Ganimard's office at the Sûreté

AT RISE, Ganimard's Secretary is seated before his table doing a jigsaw puzzle.

> SECRETARY
>
> Ah! This puzzle is truly a charming invention. What a delightful pastime on office hours.
> (looking at his watch)
> The Devil! Already 11:30 a.m. and Monsieur Ganimard telegraphed me he'd be back from Le Havre before noon. I've only got a quarter of an hour. Let's see. Where does this imposing piece belong?

The office door opens. An Office Boy enters. The Secretary hides his puzzle and pretends to pore over a file.

> SECRETARY
>
> What? What's wrong? Can't I get two minutes' peace and quiet to work?

> OFFICE BOY
>
> Monsieur Gottlieb asks to speak to you.

> SECRETARY
>
> (low)
> Let him go to the Devil.
> (aloud, surly)
> Well, show him in.

OFFICE BOY
(aside)
He's grumpy enough. I probably woke him up.

Gottlieb is shown in.

GOTTLIEB
(feverishly)
Good morning, Monsieur. Has Monsieur Ganimard arrived?

SECRETARY

Not yet.

GOTTLIEB
And, will he return soon?

SECRETARY

I don't know.

Gottlieb sits down.

GOTTLIEB
That's all right. I will wait for him. I have nothing to do all day.

SECRETARY
(aside)
Oh, damn! I'll never finish my puzzle today.

Loud voices are heard in the antechamber. Gottlieb leaps up from his chair.

GOTTLIEB
I seem to recognize his voice. He's back at last!

Ganimard appears, dressed for a trip, very agitated. Gottlieb runs towards him.

GOTTLIEB
Ah, my dear Monsieur Ganimard, I've been waiting for you impatiently. Well, is it done?

Ganimard removes his overcoat, umbrella and hat; he still looks furious.

GOTTLIEB
What's wrong with you? You seem really unnerved.

GANIMARD
Furious, I am furious. Here I am, Ganimard, Chief Inspector of the Sûreté, the best detective in France. I've been had! Arsène Lupin has kept me waiting for him in vain.

GOTTLIEB
You didn't arrest him?

GANIMARD
No. Since he didn't show up. Ah, what are we coming to if I cannot even rely on what he wrote me?

GOTTLIEB
It's frightening.

GANIMARD
(more calmly)
Still, even though this was a useless journey, it's of no great importance…

GOTTLIEB
(stupefied)
You really think so?

GANIMARD

Obviously! If Lupin wasn't in Le Havre, it's because
he's still in Paris, and if he's in Paris, I won't give
him two days before he's arrested.

GOTTLIEB

You already told me that the day before yesterday.

GANIMARD
(imperturbable)

That proves that I have steadiness of mind, which is
the main characteristic of a good policeman.

GOTTLIEB

But, you've already been running after Lupin for six
months without being able to nab him.

GANIMARD

So much the better! That's six months less I'll have
to look for him.

GOTTLIEB

Ah, I beg you, Monsieur Ganimard. Please, hurry. Do
the impossible! All the papers since yesterday morning are full of this scandal–and I ask myself how
they've learned it.

GANIMARD

Through me!

GOTTLIEB

What do you mean, through me?

GANIMARD

Naturally. Do you think that I intend to make my life
more difficult by keeping things under wrap?

GOTTLIEB
Well, then, thanks to you, I'm in a pretty difficult position now. When Nazir Pasha learns the truth, I will be ruined. My title of Prince and my commission as Admiral are lost, and Rebecca's marriage is ruined, too, for this morning, Nazir asked me for her hand.

GANIMARD
(with assurance)
Don't torment yourself! Within two days Lupin will be under lock and key. Word of Ganimard.

GOTTLIEB
From your lips to God's ears.

GANIMARD
Of course!

Ganimard pushes Gottlieb out.

GANIMARD
Oh, I will nab the rascal, Lupin! I don't know when, or how, but I will nab him.

SECRETARY
(pointing to the files)
Here are the files, Chief Inspector.

GANIMARD
That's good.
(examining the files)
Nothing interesting–some thefts–a murder! For the thefts, you will rearrange them in chronological order.

SECRETARY

Understood. What about the murder?

GANIMARD

You will wait to begin the investigation until the murderer comes forward.

SECRETARY

Very well, Chief Inspector.

The Secretary leaves. Someone knocks at the door.

GANIMARD

Enter!

The Office Boy enters.

OFFICE BOY

Chief Inspector?

GANIMARD

What is it this time?

OFFICE BOY

There are two employees from the Ministry of Fine Arts to see you.

GANIMARD

The Ministry of Fine Arts? What do they want? Well, I might as well see them. Let them in.

At a sign from the Office Boy, Fouinard, dressed as a workman, enters, followed by Lupin, similarly dressed. Each carries a modern-style armchair.

GANIMARD

What do you characters want?

Fouinard shows him a piece of paper.

> FOUINARD
> Here's the papers.

> GANIMARD
> (reading)
> "*By decree of the Ministry of Fine Arts dated June
> 17th, all furniture of historic value found in Govern-
> ment offices must be removed and sent to the State
> Museum–then replaced with modern furniture.*" Well,
> what's this got to do with me?

> FOUINARD
> Please turn the page.

> GANIMARD
> (turning the page and reading)
> "*Prefecture of Police–Office of Chief Inspector
> Ganimard. Two Empire chairs to be removed.*"
> (furious)
> What's this mean? They're going to take my chairs?
> And, without even having consulted me! It's unheard
> of.

> FOUINARD
> Then, we can take them?

> GANIMARD
> (furious)
> Since it's the Minister's order. Ah, wait, I prefer to
> not to see this.

He prepares to leave the room. Fouinard extends his hand
looking for a tip.

GANIMARD

You must be joking. Damn! Try to hurry! What a regime!

He goes into his private office. Fouinard looks for the chairs, and finds them.

FOUINARD

Ah! There they are.

LUPIN

Beautiful! They'll look nice in my office. Well, take them and go!

FOUINARD

What about you, boss? Are you going to remain here?

LUPIN

Don't concern yourself with that.

FOUINARD

All right!
        (aside)
He's got some nerve!

Fouinard carries out the two chairs while Lupin sits at Ganimard's desk. He removes his disguise and changes his face to that of Lupin.

Ganimard returns with a book.

GANIMARD

Just in case, I'm going to reread Vidocq's *Memoirs*! Perhaps I'll find an idea there. But that would surprise me! The old policemen were so lacking in imagination…

He notices Lupin sitting at his desk, rifling through the files, his back turned towards him.

>   GANIMARD
> Well, say–don't inconvenience yourself! What are you doing there rummaging through my files?

Lupin turns around.

>   LUPIN
> Ah, finally, you're here.

>   GANIMARD
>   (stupefied)
> Monsieur le Préfet de Police!

>   LUPIN
> I'm very displeased with you, Ganimard.

>   GANIMARD
>   (shaking)
> With me?

>   LUPIN
> It's been six months now that you've been running after Lupin without being able to catch him. And I am the one who is ridiculed in the press. Well, I've gotten tired of being mocked in the papers. This has got to end.

>   GANIMARD
> Monsieur le Préfet, I assure you–

>   LUPIN
> Enough excuses already! And why are you shaking like a leaf?

GANIMARD

(still shaking)

I don't know, Monsieur. It must be my legs. They're like rubber.

LUPIN

Well, sit down.

GANIMARD

Yes, Monsieur.

Ganimard falls into one of the armchairs brought earlier by Lupin and Fouinard. Immediately, it snaps into a contraption that immobilizes his arms and legs and gags him, making it impossible for him to cry out.

Lupin gets up to taunt his enemy.

LUPIN

There we are! The great Ganimard is trapped–and by whom? By Arsène Lupin! Yes, indeed, my good friend, here I am! But you don't look happy to see me? What a sour puss!

There is a knock on the door.

LUPIN

Damn! I'm sorry, Chief Inspector, but I've got to hide you for the moment.

Lupin throws a sheet on Ganimard, then returns behind the desk and assumes the face of the Secretary.

LUPIN

Come in.

The Office Boy enters.

OFFICE BOY
There's a Mister Sherlock Holmes who asks to speak
to you, Monsieur.

LUPIN
Show him in.
>(aside)

Ah, I was really hoping he would come.

The Office Boy goes to the door and introduces Sherlock
Holmes, who enters in traveling costume, his valise in his
hand. The Office Boy withdraws.

HOLMES
Monsieur.

LUPIN
>(grumpily)

Yes. What is it that you want?
>(aside)

That's good. I'm going to get him.
>(to Holmes)

Please sit down.

HOLMES
Thank you.

Holmes sits in the second chair brought earlier by Lupin and
Fouinard and is taken in the same manner as Ganimard.

Lupin, acting very friendly, gets up and removes his disguise.

LUPIN
Excuse me, my dear Mister Holmes, for employing
such a crude method with you, but I must absolutely
be guaranteed to be free of your interference tonight.
You see, I've found Miss Clark, she's not married

LUPIN (cont'd)

and I believe she still loves me. By tomorrow, I hope to convince her to leave with me and, thanks to the sale of the Sultan Diamond, we can go live in some country and lead the life of Nabobs. And now that I've kept you up to date, goodbye, my friend. Oh! Pardon, I was going to be guilty of unforgivable impoliteness…

He removes the sheet, revealing Ganimard.

LUPIN (cont'd)

Mister Holmes, may I introduce Chief Inspector Ganimard. Monsieur Ganimard, this is my friend Mister Sherlock Holmes, the famous consulting detective. As for me, gentlemen, you both know me as Arsène Lupin, Gentleman Burglar. Now that the introductions have been made, all that is left for me is to retire. I'll give orders that no one is to come in here and disturb you. You're in conference!

Lupin puts back his Secretary disguise and prepares to leave.

LUPIN (cont'd)

Ah, I almost forgot. If you need to see me, tonight I will be at Luna Park. Now I must dash! Goodbye!

Lupin leaves. We hear the sound of a key being turned in the door, then his departing footsteps.

After a few seconds, the suitcase Holmes placed on the ground opens and Frederick comes out.

FREDERICK

Decidedly this Lupin lacks imagination.

After searching the room to see if there are any more traps, Frederick goes to the armchair in which his father is strapped, finds its hidden spring, pushes it and releases Holmes.

HOLMES
All right.

Holmes gets up calmly, shakes his arms and legs and examines the armchair.

HOLMES
Very ingenious, this mechanism. Look here, Frederick.

FREDERICK
The mechanism is really simple.

HOLMES
Yes, indeed. And now, Frederick, what will you do next?

FREDERICK
I must think.

HOLMES
Very good. One must always think.

FREDERICK
Ah! Poor Monsieur Ganimard! We've forgotten him.

HOLMES
That's not important.

FREDERICK
All the same, I think he should be released.

HOLMES

As you wish.

Frederick releases Ganimard who rises, furiously.

GANIMARD
(seething)
Ah! This is too much. I'm mad as Hell.

He runs towards the door. Holmes stops him.

HOLMES
Where are you going, Chief Inspector?

GANIMARD
What do you mean, where am I going? I am going to
send my men after Lupin!

HOLMES
He locked the door.

Ganimard shakes the door, beside himself with rage.

GANIMARD
It's true, I am always locked in–I am–I am choking
with rage.

HOLMES
Don't make yourself sick, Chief Inspector. I will
open the door–when necessary.

GANIMARD
It's necessary now! Haven't you heard him? Lupin
said he would be at Luna Park tonight.

HOLMES
You really mean to arrest Lupin?

GANIMARD
Of course! What other course of action is there?

HOLMES
A *smart* course of action.

FREDERICK
Something clever, for example.

Ganimard grows red in the face and goes to Frederick.

GANIMARD
Say, little brat, I'm going to pull your ears.

Frederick adopts the stance of a boxer preparing to engage his opponent.

FREDERICK
You may try.

HOLMES
(smiling)
Be careful, Chief Inspector. Frederick's quite a boxer, you know.

Ganimard laughs disdainfully.

FREDERICK
Here, old man.

He delivers a solid blow to Ganimard, who staggers. The Chief Inspector rubs himself.

GANIMARD
That urchin of yours knows how to deliver a punch, that's for sure.

HOLMES
(calmly)

What I meant, Monsieur Ganimard, was that it would
be clumsy to arrest Lupin now, because he alone can
lead us to the Sultan Diamond.

GANIMARD

Bah! That's all rubbish from England. Me, I arrest
them first–and then afterwards, I sort out the rest.

HOLMES

If that is your method, it's not mine.

FREDERICK

Nor mine!

GANIMARD

Then we'll each work in our own way. I don't need
anyone's help.

He goes to the door, tries to open it, realizes that it's still
locked and then returns meekly to Holmes.

GANIMARD

Er, will you loan me your picklocks?

HOLMES

Gladly.

Frederick laughs, mockingly. Ganimard goes to pull his ears,
but the teenager resumes his boxing stance.

Ganimard shrugs, goes to the door, opens it and then, stands in
the doorway.

GANIMARD

Gentlemen–tonight, I will arrest Arsène Lupin. Goodbye.

Ganimard leaves.

HOLMES

Let's go, Frederick. At 9 p.m., we have an appointment at Luna Park.

CURTAIN

Scene VI
Luna Park

Luna Park at night. In the back, a set of monumental doors lead to the entrance to the establishment. To the left, the rollercoaster known as "Russian Mountains" flash with illuminated garlands. To the right, boats descend with dizzying speed from the "Waterfall" to land in a pool entirely surrounded by flag-studded arcades and decorated with multicolored electric lamps. To the right and left, the many other attractions of Luna Park are profiled.

AT RISE, a party is in full swing–amidst gales of screams and laughter. An employee of the park sends small blasts of compressed air under women's skirts, which then bellow up while the girls utter startled screams.

VARIOUS
More! More!

PARTY-GOER
These skirts aren't flying high enough. Use more air.

LUNA PARK EMPLOYEE
No can do. If I release all the pressure, it would overturn a regiment.

LARGE PARTY-GOER
Rubbish! Try knocking me over. I challenge you.

LUNA PARK EMPLOYEE
OK! You asked for it.

The Employee releases all the pressure. The large gentleman is knocked to the ground and bounces several times while everybody laughs. The Employee stops the compressed air.

While the large gentleman is being picked up and dusted off, an elegant gentleman, wearing a monocle and mustaches, enters. He is accompanied by a teenager dressed as a little huntsman. The gentleman is Sherlock Holmes and his companion is Frederick. They walk so no one can hear them.

HOLMES

Well?

FREDERICK

Lupin has been here for 15 minutes.

HOLMES

Fine. Our plan is simple, then. Ganimard is going to try to arrest him. Naturally, Lupin will slip between his fingers. There are two exits to watch. You keep an eye on one, I'll take care of the other. I'll be curious to know where he'll lead us tonight.

FREDERICK

Me too.
(loudly)
Postcards, Monsieur? Five *sous*.

HOLMES

(equally loudly)
I'll take two. Here.

FREDERICK

Thanks, Monsieur!

They each go different ways.

Nazir Pasha suddenly arrives, with a little monkey in India rubber under his arm. He is very drunk and stumbles as he walks. The Party-Goers all recognize him.

PARTY-GOERS
Ah! Nazir Pasha! There's Nazir Pasha. Hello, Nazir!

NAZIR
Hello, boys, hello. I'm very pleased to see you. I was looking for you to tell you a most extraordinary thing. Something you surely wouldn't have noticed if I didn't tell you.

FEMALE PARTY-GOER
What's that?

NAZIR
I'm smashed.

FEMALE PARTY-GOER
I think we sort of suspected it.

NAZIR
No. That's not what I meant. What I want to tell you is–I'm married.

PARTY-GOERS
Really? That's not possible! Incredible!

NAZIR
I wrote my fiancée to ask her to come and meet me here. You'll see if she isn't pretty. A real white woman. And her hair! Oh, what beautiful hair she has.

Nazir nearly trips and falls. General laughter. At the same moment, the Orchestra attacks a very joyous tune.

NAZIR

What's that? The Mazurka? The Polka?

FEMALE PARTY-GOER

No, you lug! It's the Lupin Waltz.

NAZIR

The Lupin Waltz?

FEMALE PARTY-GOER

Yes. The latest dance, what?

NAZIR

Well then, all in place for the Lupin Waltz! I will
lead!

ALL

Three cheers for Nazir!

The Lupin Waltz begins. In the midst of the dance, everybody
starts shouting: "Nazir! Nazir!" His fez askew, Nazir capers
about with great agility to a concert of foot stamping and ap-
plause. Finally, the dance ends.

PARTY-GOER

And now, to the Russian Mountains!

ALL

To the Russian Mountains!

The merry band drags Nazir along, despite his feeble attempts
at resistance, and dances off.

At that moment, Arsène Lupin appears, with Maud entering
from the other side.

LUPIN

How happy I am to have found you again, my dearest
Maud. Listen! Before, I was but a poor man and I
didn't have the right to aspire to your hand. But today, I'm rich, very rich. You remember that oath we
exchanged two years ago, on a beautiful night like
this one–do you wish to renew it tonight?

MAUD

Patience, my friend. It's been two years since we've
been separated. Give me some time. I want to be
certain that that separation has not changed your
feelings.

LUPIN

Oh! Maud, I swear to you that I love you more now
than anything else in the world. Let's take a trip–a
real American honeymoon. You'll have time to get to
know me well–and I'm sure, at the end of it, you'll
grant me your hand.

MAUD

Well, if you insist! But I must warn you–I can't leave
for two weeks.

LUPIN

Why?

MAUD

Because I've got to order new dresses, my friend. For
a woman, that's sacred. Ah, but it's late, I must go
home.

LUPIN

Would you like me to escort you to your carriage?

MAUD

No, my friend, stay. I see the friends with whom I came. I'll go with them.

Lupin kisses her hand.

LUPIN

I adore you.

MAUD

Till tomorrow.

She departs.

LUPIN

Till tomorrow.
(alone)
Another three days to struggle. Well, so be it!

Suddenly, he notices Ganimard prowling around, accompanied by his fellow policeman, Sergeant Folenfant.

LUPIN

Ganimard? If he's free, then Holmes is loose, too!! Damn!

Lupin dons a false mustache and nose and steps closer to the policemen to spy on their conversation.

GANIMARD

I've had enough of Arsène Lupin, Folenfant. But happily, this time he'll no longer escape me.

FOLENFANT

(skeptical)
You think so, Chief Inspector?

GANIMARD

Certain! Now that he's been stupid enough to show me his true face, I'll recognize him in a million.

FOLENFANT

Then, you've got a plan?

GANIMARD

(condescending)

Do I have a plan? Yes, Sergeant, I do have a plan. A plan which is entirely mine. My plan, my very own plan!

FOLENFANT

Really?

GANIMARD

Folenfant, if tonight, as every night, everyone can enter Luna Park freely, no one, you hear me, no one can leave without my permission. All exits are guarded. Once I've unmasked Lupin, I'll blow my whistle, and my men will leap on him from every side. What do you say to that?

FOLENFANT

Stunning, Chief Inspector.

LUPIN

(aside)

One whistle and all the police will run here. Perfect. There's the way to free up the exits.

GANIMARD

And now, let's go hunting, Sergeant!

He pulls a false nose out of his pocket.

GANIMARD
To approach Lupin unsuspected, I'm going to put on
this false nose which will render me unrecognizable
without attracting any attention.

FOLENFANT
That's marvelous, Chief Inspector.

GANIMARD
A half turn, Sergeant.

Folenfant makes a half turn as Ganimard puts on his nose.

GANIMARD
Another half turn, Sergeant.

Folenfant makes a half turn back.

GANIMARD
Well? What do you think?

FOLENFANT
I would never have recognized you, Chief Inspector.

GANIMARD
Indeed.

Lupin approaches, wearing a disguise.

LUPIN
(casually)
Bonsoir, Monsieur Ganimard.

GANIMARD
Ah, drats! Now what!?

LUPIN

Oh, don't be so surprised. I knew it was you all along.

GANIMARD

Really?

LUPIN

Yes. As I know that, at this very moment, you're looking for Arsène Lupin.

GANIMARD

Impossible. How could you?…

LUPIN

Easy! Here–have a look over there. It's him!

Ganimard and Folenfant stare in the direction in which he is pointing.

GANIMARD

Where?

Meanwhile, Lupin quickly removes his own mustache and false nose. When Ganimard turns around, he finds himself nose to (false) nose with his foe.

LUPIN

Here–right in front of you!

GANIMARD

(startled)

Lupin!

(to Folenfant)

Grab him!

He whistles. Policemen come from all around and seek to rush Lupin, but he pulls a revolver.

GANIMARD
Arrest him! It's Arsène Lupin!

POLICEMEN
Arsène Lupin!

The policemen again intend to rush Lupin, but he trains his revolver on them, which makes everyone recoil–then he steps aside and grabs the pipe of compressed air.

GANIMARD
Charge!

All the policemen rush Lupin, but he releases the compressed air, which knocks them over.

At the same moment, Gottlieb and Rebecca appear. Rebecca, noticing Nazir, rushes forward and is caught in a current of compressed air, which blows off her hat and wig. Lupin continues to ventilate them and bowls them over. Then, he stops, laughs and escapes. The policemen get up pitifully, rubbing their sides and rush after Lupin, limping.

Nazir sees Rebecca without her hair. He remains petrified as he picks up her wig.

NAZIR
Curses! The comet's tail was but a wig!

The Party-Goers return with paper flowers, etc. It all ends in an uproarious dance.

CURTAIN

Act III

Scene VII
Prince Mirand's office

All sides covered with glass cabinets filled with art objects. AT RISE, Baptiste, an old servant, is busy straightening up when "John" (Fouinard) enters.

FOUINARD

Hello, Baptiste.

BAPTISTE

Hello, John!

FOUINARD

Tell the boss I'm here. He sent for me.

BAPTISTE
(indignant)
I will inform His Highness.
(aside)
How vulgar this lad is! How can His Highness keep such people!

Fouinard flops down in an armchair.

FOUINARD
(yawning)
There's no sense making folks get up at such an early hour. It's hardly 8 a.m. I haven't slept 12 hours. On a regimen like this, I'm going to get sick, that's for sure.

He falls back to sleep. Lupin enters.

LUPIN

Ah, there you are at last. Why are you sleeping?

FOUINARD
(drowsy)

Hmm?

Lupin shakes him.

LUPIN

Wake up, animal!

Fouinard wakes up and leaps to his feet, trembling.

FOUINARD

Oh, damn! The boss!

LUPIN

That's better! You're going to send this telegram to my Master of the Hunt, to inform him that I will hunt tomorrow at Villiers-Cotterets, and that I will probably spend the night down there.

FOUINARD

OK, boss.

LUPIN

I've already forbidden you to call me that. I want you to call me "Your Highness" like the other servants, understood?

FOUINARD

Yes, boss–yes, Your Highness. Yes, Your Highness boss. Oh, how difficult this is.

Lupin gives him several letters.

LUPIN

Here are some letters that you will deliver in person.
They're invitations for the hunt. This way, they'll get
there quicker. I especially recommend this one. Pay
close attention.

FOUINARD

Don't worry.
(reading the address)
Miss Clark, Electric Hotel.

Fouinard puts it in his pocket. There is a pause. Then:

LUPIN

Have you learned anything new regarding Holmes'
whereabouts?

FOUINARD

Absolutely nothing. Since he escaped from Ganimard's office, nothing! Impossible to discover his
tracks. I guess he's had enough after his first en-
counter with you–and he's left for England.

LUPIN

Him! Give up? You don't know him. He never lets
go of his prey–especially when this prey is Arsène
Lupin. It would be madness to appear under my real
face now. He knows it too well. I must remain Prince
Mirand for the time being, because he, at least, is
sheltered from all suspicions.

Lupin takes a cigarette from the table and lights it. Fouinard,
in imitation, does the same.

FOUINARD

I agree.

Lupin calls him to order.

> LUPIN
> And mind your manners!

> FOUINARD
> Yes, yes! I'll go and smoke in the kitchen, with
> the other servants.

He puts the cigarette in his pocket.

> FOUINARD
> But, what are you going to do about Miss Clark?

> LUPIN
> Nothing could be simpler. Prince Mirand cannot be
> seen to be connected with Miss Clark; however, it
> happens that he received a letter from a friend–which
> will turn out to be a forgery, if one examines it
> closely–asking him to invite her to his hunt. Prince
> Mirand has therefore no reason not do so. And at
> Villiers-Cotterets, it'll be easy for me to appear under
> the features of either Prince Mirand–or André
> Largery.

> FOUINARD
> (admiringly)
> Ah, you think of everything!

> LUPIN
> I try. Yet, I'll confess to you, Fouinard, that I'm
> worried for the first time in my life.

> FOUINARD
> How can that be? Until now, you've mocked
> everyone and everything.

LUPIN

That's because until now, I was only risking my free-dom. Today, it's my happiness that's at stake. Ah, I'd like to be two days older. By then, Sherlock Holmes will have returned to England and I'll have nothing to fear anymore. But, until then... Heavens, I ask my-self all the time if that Devil of a man isn't going to spring from a trap and suddenly appear before me.

FOUINARD

Oh, there's no risk. We're not at the Opera.

Someone knocks at the door.

LUPIN

Enter.

Baptiste enters with a card on a silver tray. Lupin examines it with emotion.

LUPIN

Show him in.

Baptiste goes back out.

FOUINARD

Who is it?

LUPIN

Sherlock Holmes.

FOUINARD
(shaking)
Sherlock Holmes? Oh, my God! For sure, he's come to arrest us.

LUPIN

We shall soon find out.

FOUINARD

What? You are going to see him?

LUPIN

Why not? Quick, step into my office.

FOUINARD

(running)

Oh, yes!

LUPIN

And don't lose a word of what is said.

FOUINARD

Yes, boss! No, boss! Oh, why couldn't he remain in
his own country, the beast.

Fouinard leaves, going into the office by which Lupin entered.
Lupin sits and pretends to read. Baptiste introduces Sherlock
Holmes.

HOLMES

I beg you to excuse me, Prince Mirand, if I present
myself to you at such an early hour.

LUPIN

You are completely excused, dear sir. Baptiste, pull
up a chair…

Baptiste pulls up a chair and leaves. Holmes sits down.

LUPIN (cont'd)

I'm really delighted to make your acquaintance,
Mister Holmes. I've often heard of you, and the tales

LUPIN (cont'd)
of your exploits have always fascinated me to the
highest degree.

HOLMES
Your Highness is too kind.

LUPIN
Not at all! Not at all. Fascinate is the word.

HOLMES
Then, I'm doubly happy, for I'm going to tell you of
a new and very curious adventure upon which I've
embarked, one that will interest you all the more because, without your suspecting it, you're personally
involved in it.

LUPIN
Me?

HOLMES
Yes. I'm counting on you to help me lift one of the
veils under which the mysterious Arsène Lupin hides
himself.

LUPIN
Really?

HOLMES
Indeed. And see how astonishing everything is that
concerns this puzzling character–do you know where
he is hiding at this very moment?

LUPIN
My word, no.

HOLMES

Right here, Your Highness, in your mansion.

LUPIN

That's impossible.

HOLMES

I'm as sure of it as that we are both here together.

LUPIN

Mercy! Please explain yourself quickly, Mister
Holmes, for I ask myself if I'm not dreaming.

HOLMES

Arsène Lupin, after having spent the evening at Luna
Park, left that playground around 11:15 p.m. He took
a cab which took him to Avenue Friedland. There, he
settled the fare and walked down the Avenue until he
reached the Rue Balzac, turning from time to time to
see if he wasn't being followed. Finally, he arrived at
No. 18 of this street. There, he pulled out a key from
his pocket, opened a small door, well hidden in the
wall of your mansion, and entered.

LUPIN

Truly, Mister Holmes, you see me stupefied. Arsène
Lupin entered my mansion through a secret door?
Now, that is upsetting indeed. May I ask how you
know all this?

HOLMES

Very easily. My son Frederick, who is small and ag-
ile, leaped on the rear of the cab. After Lupin got out,
he followed him, carefully hiding behind the trees.
He saw him enter by this secret door, the existence of
which was unknown to you and which opens into a
stall in your stables.

LUPIN

Come on!

HOLMES

Frederick waited around for a half-hour, then spying another cab, he gave the driver a franc to go and fetch me from a place we'd agreed on in advance. We spent the whole night on guard. Since no one has yet left, either through the big door or by the little door, and as there is no other exit, Lupin is still here. That's all.

LUPIN

This is truly a story worthy of the Arabian Nights! I can't get over your cleverness.

HOLMES

Mere child's play, Your Highness.

LUPIN

What do you plan to do now? Search the hotel from top to bottom, doubtless?

HOLMES

No.

LUPIN

Would you like me to call my people so you could question them?

HOLMES

Please don't do that. That would be the best way of not finding anything out.

LUPIN

What, then?

HOLMES

I'll simply ask you to grant me permission to walk in your hotel under the guise of admiring your marvelous art collection. That will enable me to speak to your staff without awakening suspicions.

LUPIN

Of course.

Lupin rings. Baptiste enters.

LUPIN

Baptiste, this gentleman desires to visit the hotel. You are to let him go wherever he wishes.

BAPTISTE

Yes, Your Highness.

LUPIN

Excuse me for not escorting you myself, Mister Holmes, but I have a meeting at 10 a.m.

HOLMES

It's I who must apologize for disturbing you.

LUPIN

I hope, indeed, to have the pleasure of talking with you at greater length later.

HOLMES

It will be a great honor for me, Your Highness.

Holmes bows and leaves, followed by Baptiste. Lupin steps forward with an angry gesture. Fouinard comes out of the office.

LUPIN

You heard?

FOUINARD

Everything!

LUPIN

He's a fearsome adversary, that Sherlock Holmes.

FOUINARD

You think that he suspects you?

LUPIN

Not yet, but within the hour he will know that Lupin and Prince Mirand are one and the same.

FOUINARD

Good Lord! Then, we're finished.

LUPIN

Perhaps… Unless…
          (a pause, then smiling to himself)
I think I've just found a way to cut short his investigation.

FOUINARD

How's that?

LUPIN

By causing Arsène Lupin to be arrested.

FOUINARD

You–?

LUPIN

In person.

FOUINARD

Ah, my God! My boss has gone mad!

LUPIN

(plotting)

Yes, yes, that's it. Once Arsène Lupin is under lock and key, Sherlock Holmes will stop his pursuit and then Prince Mirand and André Largery will be able to move safely. Yes, there's no other way.

FOUINARD

You're really serious, boss? You're going to get yourself arrested by Sherlock Holmes?

LUPIN

Get myself arrested? Yes, but not by Sherlock Holmes.

FOUINARD

By whom then?

LUPIN

By that faithful and devoted friend who is always about whenever I need to get me out of a tricky spot– by that excellent Monsieur Ganimard.

FOUINARD

(astonished)

Ganimard!

(hitting his forehead)

I'm with you now, boss. With that one, there's no risks of errors. Ah, what a great guy you are!

Lupin grabs the telephone.

LUPIN

Hello! Hello!

FOUINARD

What are you doing, boss?

LUPIN

I'm calling Ganimard. Hello, please give me 515-53.

FOUINARD

He ought to be in his office already.

LUPIN

Hello? Is this the office of Chief Inspector Gani-
mard? Ah, you're his secretary? Is the Chief Inspec-
tor there? No?
      (aside)
Damn! This is very annoying.
      (to telephone)
It's a matter of the highest importance, pertaining to
Arsène Lupin! What's that. you say? Ah! Fine! Fine!
Very fine, thanks.

Lupin hangs up the telephone.

FOUINARD

Well, boss?

LUPIN

Ganimard is presently on official business at the Police Station of the Champs-Elysées.

FOUINARD

Why, that's just two steps from here.

LUPIN

Go and bring him to me, dead or alive.

FOUINARD

Don't worry. In three minutes, I'll be back with him.

LUPIN

You'll take him here. Then, you'll come and warn me. I'll be in my office.

FOUINARD

Right!

LUPIN

One last thing! It's necessary that the driver Ganimard will requisition to take me to the station be one of our men. Once we arrive at the corner of the Rue de Richelieu and the Boulevards, it's play No. 3. Understood?

FOUINARD

Understood!

LUPIN

Go then!

Fouinard leaves. Lupin goes towards his office, then he stops. He goes to a desk and opens a drawer.

LUPIN

I almost forgot.
          (pulling out a map)
This map of the forest of Villiers-Cotterets. It must fall into Holmes' hands. He'll know what to do with…

One hears voices in the distance.

LUPIN

Ganimard already? With him, it's really too easy!

He quickly goes into his office. Just then, Ganimard rushes into the room with two policemen.

> GANIMARD
>
> Where is Lupin? Where is he so I can put the cuffs on him?

> FOUINARD
>
> If you keep shouting like that, Monsieur Ganimard, you're going to help him get away.

> GANIMARD
>
> You're right!

> FOUINARD
>
> Naturally! The best thing for you to do is to wait and nab him right here when he returns to steal all those wonderful objets d'art. You understand?

> GANIMARD
>
> I've got it!
>   (to his men)
> Folenfant, hide behind that armchair. You, Dieuzy, behind this sofa! And, as for me, there.
>   (pointing to the desk)
> The center of operations.

He plunges under the desk.

> FOUINARD
>
> Great! Say, Chief Inspector, what if I went to find a cab to take Lupin in after you've arrested him?

> GANIMARD
>
> Good idea, my boy. Hurry up, because I've got the notion this isn't going to take long.

FOUINARD

Now I'm going to warn the boss. Oh, no, they'll never make another policeman like that one.

GANIMARD

Hush! Are you there?

POLICEMEN

Yes, Chief Inspector.

GANIMARD

Don't make any noise. That's of the greatest importance.

POLICEMEN

Yes, Chief Inspector.

Silence, then a formidable sneeze.

GANIMARD
(shouting)
Will you shut up, Folenfant?

FOLENFANT

It's not my fault, it's my head cold.

GANIMARD

When you're on duty, you leave your cold at home.

FOLENFANT

Right, Chief Inspector.

A silence. Jolts from the couch.

GANIMARD

Dieuzy, what are you doing with that sofa?

DIEUZY
I've got a cramp, Chief Inspector.

GANIMARD
A cramp! A cramp! I'll give you a cramp! Button up!

DIEUZY
Right, Chief Inspector.

At this moment, the door of the room opens quietly.

GANIMARD
Hush!

Lupin appears, dressed as he was at Luna Park. He crouches against the wall, in a mock-burglar pose, and puts some trinkets in his pocket. Then he tiptoes exaggeratedly towards the door. Ganimard grabs his foot, but Lupin grabs his neck and chokes him in the struggle.

GANIMARD
I've got him! I've got him! Help me! Thief! Thief!

The men rush forward and force Lupin to release Ganimard. All the servants in the hotel arrive.

GANIMARD
Ah, my little Lupin! Yesterday, they made fun of old Ganimard. But today, he who laughs last, laughs best.

Sherlock Holmes enters. Ganimard notices him.

GANIMARD
Ah, it's you, Mister Consulting Detective. As you can see, I'm the one who nabbed Lupin after all. Sorry to have to disappoint you.

HOLMES

Indeed. Especially because I think you've made a serious mistake.

GANIMARD

Yes, I know, your system. But, it's not mine!
(to Baptiste)
Please inform Prince Mirand that I wish to see him.

BAPTISTE

I'm afraid His Highness left a few minutes ago.

GANIMARD

Too bad! I would have liked for him to have been present during all this. That would have given me a bit of fame. Anyway...
(to his men)
Search him!

They search Lupin.

FOLENFANT

A gold snuffbox, two watches and two tie pins.

GANIMARD

That's fine. That's very fine. We have more than we need as evidence for a conviction.

DIEUZY
(holding a folded map)
Chief Inspector, there was also this in his pocket.

GANIMARD

What's this? A map? The gentleman drives a motor car, I bet! These thieves can refuse themselves nothing.

He crumples it up.

> GANIMARD
> Might as well throw it away.

Holmes steps forward.

> HOLMES
> Would you give it to me? As a souvenir! It will re-
> mind me of your brilliant exploit.

Ganimard gives the map to Holmes.

> GANIMARD
> Gladly!
> > (to Lupin)
> And now, off to the station and no back talk or I'll
> give you a taste of the brass knuckles.

Lupin leaves, escorted by the policemen and followed by servants.

> GANIMARD
> > (to Holmes)
> No hard feelings, Mister Consulting Detective?

> HOLMES
> I assure you, it's impossible to wish you ill, Chief In-
> spector

> GANIMARD
> > (aside, laughing)
> Ha! He is jealous.

He leaves.

HOLMES

Arsène Lupin arrested by Ganimard, that's not to be
believed.
(unfolding the map)
A map of the Forest of Villiers-Cotterets… What are
these? Two little blue crosses… There's something
written underneath… *Nine steps from King
Dagobert–at a height of two tiers–a hole covered
with moss–place the key in it and it will open...* What
can this mean? Could it be–?

Frederick rushes in.

FREDERICK

Oh, Papa, Papa! Have you arrested Lupin?

HOLMES

No. It was that fool Ganimard.

FREDERICK
(disappointed)
Ah! But then, since he's in prison, we'll no longer be
able to find the diamond?

HOLMES

Yes, perhaps.

FREDERICK

How?

HOLMES
(showing him the map)
With this.

Holmes and Frederick study the map.

CURTAIN

Scene VIII
Rue de Richelieu

At the back, the Rue Richelieu, which is perpendicular to the grand boulevards, which cross the stage. There is unusual traffic. A policeman with a stick stops the carriages coming from the Rue de Richelieu, which are lining up in the back, facing the public, while carriages on the boulevards are allowed to go through.

POLICEMAN

Come forward.

CAB DRIVER

Hey, Cocotte! Hey Cocotte!

The horse hardly moves into the middle of the stage when, from the other direction, a large carriage, led by Fouinard, moves into the intersection and finds itself head to head with the first carriage.

POLICEMAN

Back off, you idiot!

FOUINARD

But I'm going to the Rue de Richelieu, Officer.

POLICEMAN

Then go around.

CAB DRIVER

Yeah, go by way of the Bastille.

FOUINARD

I don't need your advice, you dimwit!

CAB DRIVER
(angry)
Dimwit? Look who's talking! He looks like a proper
village idiot!

FOUINARD

Village idiot? Well, at least, I don't look like the hind
end of a jackass!

CAB DRIVER

Jackass? Did he say, jackass? That's it! I'm getting
off! He can tell me that to my face!

POLICEMAN

Stop! Stay where you are! If you don't shut up at
once, I'll fine both of you!

FOUINARD

Why me? He started it! I was only minding my own
business when that hairy ape butted in!

CAB DRIVER

Hairy ape! By all that's holy! If I didn't control
myself...

FOUINARD
(laughing)
Come down from your seat, eh, coward!

CROWD

Come down! Stay where you are! Punch him out!
Don't give in!

A small crowd has gathered. Some take the part of the Cab Driver, others Fouinard's. Ganimard gets out of his carriage.

> GANIMARD
> What's the matter? What's going on?

> POLICEMAN
> It's this idiot who's blocking traffic.

> GANIMARD
> I am Ganimard, Chief Inspector of the Sûreté.
> Make way for us!

> POLICEMAN
> Right away, Chief Inspector!

Lupin jumps out of the cab.

> LUPIN
> Say, Ganimard, this is taking a bit too long.
> Do you mind if I go and have a beer?

> GANIMARD
> What? No!

But Lupin has already vanished into the crowd.

> GANIMARD
> Arrest him! Arrest him! It's Arsène Lupin!

> CROWD
> Arsène Lupin!

Ganimard whistles. The policemen, including the traffic warden, all rush after Lupin who has vanished. Having taken advantage of the confusion, he then reappears between the two cabs.

Lupin comes down stage, but three policemen appear from the right and four from the left, blocking his way.

He jumps into Fouinard's carriage; the policemen try to jump after him, but they are prevented by Fouinard pretending to help them. Finally, they manage to get in, but by then, Lupin has jumped out of the back.

The policemen are hot in pursuit. Lupin gets into an alley, removes his coat, reverses it and returns on stage now dressed as a policeman, having grabbed an impersonator who was waiting for him.

POLICEMAN (LUPIN)
There he is! I've got him!

The phony policeman (Lupin) hustles the false Lupin with blows and pushes him towards Ganimard's cab.

POLICEMAN (LUPIN)
This time, I bet he'll stay put!

GANIMARD
Congratulations, Agent 666. I'm Chief Inspector Ganimard, Here's a 100 francs reward.

Ganimard pulls out a 100-francs note from his billfold and gives it to the phony policeman (Lupin).

POLICEMAN (LUPIN)
You're too kind, Chief Inspector.

GANIMARD
No, no. It's worth it. As for this idiot...
(pointing to Fouinard)

GANIMARD (cont'd)
I've just checked; he's got no license for his cab. I'll
have it impounded!

POLICEMAN (LUPIN)
I'll see to it.

Ganimard gets back in his cab with the phony Lupin. An officer gets on the seat and the cab sets off.

FOUINARD
I'll going to complain to my Representative!
(low to Lupin)
Well, boss, are you pleased? This went off rather
well, didn't it?

LUPIN
You can say that again. And to reward you, here's
100 francs. Don't thank me, they're Ganimard's.

FOUINARD
A nice gesture all the same, boss.

LUPIN
Let's be off. To the Railway Station.

He drags him along the boulevard, hustling him.

POLICEMAN
Come on! Keep moving.

Pedestrians, carriages, autos, honking horns, newsboys, etc.

CURTAIN

Scene IX

The Forest at Villiers-Cotterets

In the rear, there is a large pool which, on one side, is adjacent to some ruins, with a partially broken statue in their midst. On the other side, we see a hunting lodge.

AT RISE, several horsemen and horsewomen, all dressed in hunting costume, are seated, drinking. Two servants pass a tray of champagne glasses. Some chairs and rustic benches can be seen around the back of the lodge.

GOTTLIEB
Gentlemen, a toast to Prince Mirand, the most
amiable of Hunt Masters!

ALL
(raising their glasses)
To Prince Mirand!

GOTTLIEB
The pack just took a wrong scent but the Prince
is busy raising it up.

GUEST No. 1
And with him–he's never misled.

GUEST No. 2
By the way, my dear Gottlieb, you must be happy.
Now Lupin is under lock and key.

GOTTLIEB

Er, yes. Unfortunately, when they arrested him, they
only found on him the jewels he'd just stolen from
Prince Mirand. As for my diamond–impossible to
make him tell where he's hidden it. He refuses to answer any questions.

GUEST No. 2

Damn rotten luck! But if the Sultan Diamond isn't
found, what are you going to tell Nazir Pasha?

GOTTLIEB

Ah, don't mention it. Since yesterday, I've been
completely obsessed with that. And to add to my
misfortune, Nazir has broken off his engagement to
Rebecca. And why? Because she wears a wig? Ah,
it's really too bad.

GUEST No. 1
(seeing Mirand)
Ah, here's Prince Mirand.

Mirand and Maud, dressed in hunting attire, appear.

LUPIN

Gentlemen, the scent is taken again and the stag's
just been started.

ALL

To the horses!

Several guests mount their horses and leave.

LUPIN
(to Maud)
If you don't mind, dear Madame, we're going to stop
a few moments to drink a cup of champagne and give
our horses time to breathe.

MAUD
(going to sit down)
Ah, Prince. Don't make me miss the Tally Ho!

LUPIN
(laughing)
A master huntsman, miss the Tally Ho! Ha! The only
thing left for him to do would be to commit suicide.

Mirand thanks the guests as they move away.

LUPIN
(aside)
I have to know if she really loves me–and how far her
love goes.

A valet brings some champagne for Maud at the rustic table
and pours it.

LUPIN
You don't feel too worn out, dear Madame?

MAUD
Tired, from what?

LUPIN
We've been on horseback four hours and the stag's
led us such a merry chase that we've lost half of the
huntsmen–including poor Largery who is probably
lost in the forest.

MAUD

No. He was forced to leave the hunt. A very important matter called him back to Paris. He even begged
me, being unable to talk to you, to express his regrets.

LUPIN

André is at home here. He's got nothing to apologize
for.

MAUD

Oh, he regretted leaving so much, but this boring
business of his will keep him away all day tomorrow
and we can't meet again until the night of the Amateur Circus Performers. At Monsieur Monnier's, I
believe?

LUPIN

Well I'm delighted that you came. We will certainly
see each other again there. But to get back to
Largery–it seems that you're quite interested in my
young friend.

MAUD

Prince, you risk becoming indiscreet.

LUPIN

Please! I'm like an old confidante with whom one
can, without fear, share a secret. You see, I feel a
great friendship for André, and I know he's got great
affection for you.

MAUD

Ah! He told you that?

LUPIN

No, but I had little trouble discovering it.

MAUD

So he spoke to you about me?

LUPIN

Often.

MAUD
(slightly hesitant)
And you think that he loves me? That he sincerely loves me?

LUPIN

I'm sure of it!

MAUD

What joy!

LUPIN
And you, do you love him?

MAUD
(after a slight hesitation)
Yes.

LUPIN

Very much?

MAUD

Very much.

LUPIN
How happy he would be if he heard you... A simple supposition... If, by chance, one day, you were to learn things about him, things about his past–things that might be painful to discover–would your love for him be strong enough to pardon him?

MAUD

Oh! Prince, what a strange question!

LUPIN

True, but I'd be curious to know your answer.

MAUD

Then I would tell you that André being the most honest and upright man that I know–the question will never be asked.

LUPIN

Evidently. Please, excuse me. I've been stupid to speak to you of this…

A pause. One hears hunting horns in the distance. Maud gets on her horse. As soon as Maud and Lupin are in saddle, they leave.

LUPIN

Ah, that tells us the stag is approaching. In a half-hour, it will be the Tally Ho.

As Lupin prepares to ride away, he notices Sherlock Holmes approaching.

LUPIN

(aside)

Him again.

Holmes enters, very absorbed, map in hand, counting his steps. Frederick follows him, carrying a traveler's bag

HOLMES

33, 34, 35, and 36. It's there!

FREDERICK

You think so, Papa?

HOLMES

I'm sure of it. See this statue, Frederick? It wears a crown! It's that of King Dagobert. Without doubt, we've found Lupin's lair. Nothing left to do now, except to find the way of entering it.

FREDERICK

I've brought everything necessary. A crowbar, a hammer, a screwdriver, a lantern and a rope ladder.

HOLMES

Perhaps that will be useful later. Right now, go stand guard over there–on that rock. If you notice anyone, warn me. I don't want to be surprised.

FREDERICK

Right, Papa.

He goes out.

HOLMES

(reading from the map)

"Nine steps from King Dagobert–at a height of two tiers–a hole covered with moss–place the key in it and it will open." Yes.

Holmes puts the map in his pocket, whistling. At this moment, Lupin enters the lodge and looks out the window. Night begins to fall.

Lupin opens a panel in the wall located near the window. There are four levers inside. He watches Holmes as the Detective finally locates the opening hidden under the moss.

After several tries, the King Dagobert statue turns with the panel of wall in which it is encased. As it opens, it reveals a secret passage.

                    HOLMES
                  (delighted)
          Ah! I think now that I won't be long in finding the diamond.
                  (calling)
          Frederick! Frederick!

                    FREDERICK
                  (in the distance)
          Coming, Papa!

                    HOLMES
          Let's see where this stairway leads.

As he walks back to the table to grab the lantern, Holmes' pipe falls from his pocket. The Detective does not notice it. He lights the lantern and steps into the opening.

At this moment, Lupin presses a lever and the stone panel shuts abruptly behind Holmes, trapping him inside.

                    LUPIN
          This time, I've got him! Ah, my good Mister Holmes, you wanted to know more about Arsène Lupin? Well, I am going to satisfy your curiosity…

Lupin opens a trap door in the floor of the lodge and disappears into it.

Outside, Frederick returns.

                    FREDERICK
          Here I am, Papa! Here I am.

He looks around–no Holmes in sight.

> FREDERICK
> Heavens–Papa's not here! But I'm certain I heard
> him call me.
> > (calling)
> Papa! Papa!... Nothing! What's it mean?

He then notices Holmes' pipe on the ground and picks it up.

> FREDERICK
> Papa's pipe! Surely something bad has happened to
> him!
> > (calling again)
> Papa! My Papa!... I'm afraid. I'm afraid.

He falls into a chair, weeping. A pause. Then he rises ener-
getically.

> FREDERICK
> Afraid? I? The son of Sherlock Holmes? No way!
> Papa is in danger and I will save him!

> CURTAIN

Scene X

Lupin's Lair

The stage represents the interior of a subterranean cavern. A path can barely be discerned descending amidst the jutting rocks. It's very dark. Sherlock Holmes appears at the top of the path, carefully walking down, lighting the way with his lantern.

HOLMES

Rocks, rocks everywhere! This time, I think I've reached the bottom of this cave! The Devil takes that secret door! Was it the wind that shut it behind me? Or something else? Ah, bah, I shall discover it soon enough. Let's look at this place…

He looks around, projecting his lantern's light on the rocky walls.

HOLMES

Not a soul. In fact, there's nothing here to make me believe that any human has ever set foot in this cavern. Still, I'm sure I'm not mistaken. This is Lupin's lair. That where he's hidden the Sultan Diamond.

One hears a distant growling sound.

HOLMES

Heavens! What's that?

The growling increases. Suddenly, the cavern is flooded by many, flashing red lights, giving it a somewhat Hellish look.

HOLMES

Is Satan going to some expense to receive me?

There is a formidable clap of thunder and a crimson wraith-
like figure appears at the top of the rocks, standing proud, his
arms crossed. It's Lupin. Holmes remains motionless, holding
his lantern trained on the "wraith." Lupin finally unmasks and
comes down the rocky path to meet Holmes.

LUPIN

My compliments, Mister Holmes. You've got an
admirable sense of self-control.

HOLMES

It comes with the territory, Monsieur Lupin.

LUPIN

You don't seem astonished to see me.

HOLMES

Why should I be? Weren't you in Ganimard's hands?

LUPIN
(laughing)

Yes, that explains everything, doesn't it? My first
task after having secured my freedom was to come
here, for I knew that you would find your way here
today.

HOLMES
(surprised)

Really? How?

LUPIN

Because of the map that I was careful to pocket before I got arrested, which you took from Ganimard
and which led you straight here.

HOLMES
(aside, vexed)
I've been had!
(aloud)
I see. Well, do with me what you will.

LUPIN
Oh, rest easy. Do you remember the famous Council
of Ten in Ancient Venice? Well, we're not in Venice
here, only a few leagues from Paris, but I've got my
own Council of Ten–you might call it, the partners
and associates of the enterprise known as Lupin In-
corporated.

Lupin strikes a gong. The boulders up front vanish and ten
women in red cloaks and masks enter.

HOLMES
(astonished)
Women.

LUPIN
And charming ones, I assure you! You see, my dear
Mister Holmes, in this century of airplanes, when the
art of theft has taken such flight, I can't afford to remain behind the times! The methods of the great
thieves of the past, Mandrin and Cartouche, are no
more! This is a new world. No more violence, no
more brutality. I've managed to obtain everything I
seek through beauty and grace. Formerly, when people saw a thief, they shouted: "Catch him!" I want
them to shout: "Encore!" To attain this goal, I've
employed the most seductive and irresistible means
of all–women!

151

HOLMES

Very clever.

LUPIN

I thought so. But to the charm nature has given them, I've added something else. I wanted my ladies to have strength, power. Thanks to a sophisticated training program, they're among the finest in hand-to-hand combat, marksmanship and fencing. Now is, in fact, the time of their fencing practice. You'll be able to judge their skills for yourself.

Lupin makes a gesture. The gong strikes again. The boulders turn on themselves and create a well-lit stage. Lupin gestures for Holmes to come and sit beside him.

The ten red clad, masked women then perform a ballet with a fencing theme. At the end of it, Lupin turns towards Holmes.

LUPIN

Well, Detective, what do you think of my associates?

HOLMES

That they would shame even our most accomplished swordsmen.

LUPIN
(to the dancers)
Ladies, I thank you.

At a gesture from Lupin, they leave.

LUPIN

With such auxiliaries, everything becomes easy. In a few years, I've been able to accumulate some of the world's most valuable treasures. Here, look.

Lupin makes a sign and a tapestry at the rear slides away, revealing a showcase filled with marvelous works of art.

HOLMES
(dazzled)
Oh!

LUPIN
(triumphant)
Now, there's a collection that most millionaires would envy, wouldn't they? All the famous jewels stolen during the last few years are here. There's the tiara of Saitapshanies, the real one, the Eucharist Dove, the Reliquary of Ambaze, the Statue of Isis, Miss Emilteniere d'Alenion's necklace...

HOLMES
And, in this box?

LUPIN
Millions of other things. Everything here is a worth a fortune! What are you looking for ? Ah, yes, the Sultan Diamond! Oh! I'm sorry. I took it to an expert yesterday, who hasn't yet sent it back. But, I see you distracted. What are you thinking of?

HOLMES
I'm thinking that if you had employed the admirable resources of your intelligence and your imagination in other ways, you would surely have been a great inventor or a great artist.

LUPIN
That's quite possible, but then I wouldn't have had the great pleasure of fighting Sherlock Holmes–and the greater glory of winning that fight.

HOLMES
Excuse me, but you haven't won yet.

LUPIN
What do you mean? You still hope?

HOLMES
More than hope.

LUPIN
This very afternoon, Friday, at six o'clock–

HOLMES
At six o'clock, you will be arrested.

LUPIN
(smiling)
May I remind you that it's you who are my prisoner
right now. Come, my dear Mister Holmes, give me
your word of honor that you'll return to England tonight, and I'll let you go free.

HOLMES
I regret, but I can't do that.

LUPIN
Why not?

HOLMES
Because I still intend to get the Sultan Diamond back.

LUPIN
But, how could you–?

HOLMES
I have my methods.

LUPIN

Your stubbornness saddens me more than I can say.
Won't you at least reconsider–?

HOLMES

No.

LUPIN

Then–the straitjacket.

Four men rush out and forcibly strap Holmes into a straitjacket, despite his desperate resistance. They then leave.

LUPIN

My most sincere apologies, Mister Holmes, but
you've forced me into it.

Lupin, too, leaves.

After a few seconds, Holmes begins wiggling about and,
Houdini-like, succeeds in freeing himself from the straitjacket.

He lights his lantern and looks right, then left.

HOLMES

Decidedly, there's no way out this way. I'll have to
go back the way I came. Once up there I'll find a way
to spring the secret door.

He starts going back but encounters boulders in his path.

HOLMES

How can that be? Rocks there, where I first came
from? Then I *am* a prisoner. Me, Sherlock Holmes,
defeated by Arsène Lupin!

Suddenly, stones fall almost at his feet, followed by more stones.

                    HOLMES
          Ah? What's that?
                    (looking up)
          A light?

                    FREDERICK
          Papa! Papa!

                    HOLMES
                    (moved)
          That voice.

A rope ladder drops and Frederick appears.

                    FREDERICK
          Papa! Papa! Are you there?

                    HOLMES
          Frederick! Is that you?

                    FREDERICK
                    (at the top of the ladder)
          Yes, Papa. I discovered a hollow rock and I let the
          ladder down. Here I am.

                    HOLMES
          That's fine, very fine that, Frederick.

                    FREDERICK
          Come quick.

                    HOLMES
          Oh, there's no need to hurry any more.

FREDERICK

But Lupin must be arrested on Friday before 6 p.m.!

HOLMES

He will be. For now, I know someone who can help
with our investigation.

FREDERICK

Who?

HOLMES

(smiling)

Prince Mirand.

CURTAIN

Scene XI

Backstage at Circus Monnier

It's a beehive of activity. Clowns and circus riders come and go in every direction.

FIRST RIDER
Well, my dear Monnier, are you pleased?

FEMALE CLOWN
Now, there's a truly *chic* performance.

MONNIER
I'm delighted, children, over the Moon with happiness.

He notices Nazir, loitering in the background.

MONNIER
What are you still doing here, my dear Nazir? You should be in your dressing room, preparing for the pantomime.

NAZIR
But I'm ready!

MONNIER
What about your head? And your whiskers?

NAZIR
True. I was going to forget my head.

He leaves just as Lupin, dressed as Prince Mirand, enters.

LUPIN

Ah, my dear Monnier. All my compliments. Never
have you presented us such a beautiful program.

MONNIER

Oh! Your Excellency! You're too kind!

LUPIN

No, no! I'm not exaggerating in the least. Especially
the little lady with the rabbits. She's a wonderful
idea.

MONNIER

A very Parisian observation, if you don't mind my
saying so. But you will excuse me, Your Excellency,
I've got to keep an eye on my people.

LUPIN

Go, *Cher Artiste*, go!

MONNIER

Ladies, Gentlemen, please, I beg you, go get dressed–
quickly. It's only a 20 minute intermission. Hurry!

ALL

We're going! We're going!

They leave, jostled by Monnier. Ganimard enters.

LUPIN
(watching the performers)
And they say they work for their own pleasure...
(surprised, noticing Ganimard)
What are *you* doing here, my dear Chief Inspector?

GANIMARD
(mysteriously)
Hush!

LUPIN
What's wrong?

GANIMARD
No one can hear us?

LUPIN
As you can see, we're quite alone.

GANIMARD
(importantly)
Prince Mirand, extraordinary things are going to take place here this evening.

LUPIN
Really?

GANIMARD
First of all, I must tell you that the Lupin I arrested yesterday was not the real Lupin.

LUPIN
That's impossible!

GANIMARD
And yet, it's the truth. While I was taking the real Lupin to headquarters, that rascal took advantage of a traffic jam to have himself replaced by a double.

LUPIN
That's unheard of! If I may ask... how did you find it out?

GANIMARD

Truth to tell, I didn't. Sherlock Holmes told me.

LUPIN

Ah! Sherlock Holmes... Er, when did he tell you?
Yesterday evening, doubtless?

GANIMARD

No! Today!
            (aside)
He doesn't understand anything.

LUPIN

            (aside)
Damn! He's escaped again!
            (aloud)
So you've come here to try to catch this damned
Lupin again?

GANIMARD

Yes and no. All I can tell you is that I'm here acting
on another of Holmes' suggestions. This time, I'm
supposed to arrest a woman...

LUPIN

            (astonished)
A woman?

GANIMARD

Quite a wealthy lady, too. Miss Maud Clark.

Lupin becomes very upset at the news but hides it success-
fully.

LUPIN

What's her connection with Arsène Lupin?

GANIMARD

That I don't know. That damned Englishman only
told me: 'If you arrest Miss Clark tonight, I guarantee
you that, by morning, you will have both Lupin and
the Sultan Diamond.'

LUPIN
(aside)
The wretch.

GANIMARD
(aside)
He's completely stupid.
(addressing Lupin)
I didn't really grasp what he meant, but you
understand that one arrest more or less is no great
matter. Only, to avoid any scandal, I'll arrest her before the performance resumes.

LUPIN

Yes, you're right.

GANIMARD

This is all between you and me, of course–the Englishman strongly advised me to not speak of this to
anyone. But you're being such a friend–

LUPIN

Never doubt it.

GANIMARD

Well, I'm going to go and keep an eye on my men.
Goodbye, Prince.

Ganimard leaves.

LUPIN
(alone)
That damned Detective is constantly nipping at my
feet! I understand his game. Once Maud is in his
hands, if I don't bring him the Diamond, he'll tell her
that Lupin and Largery are one and the same. But I
don't want that! I've got to snatch her away from
Ganimard. But how?...

Monnier enters quickly, followed by Sherlock Holmes,
dressed as a Circus Rider, and some clowns.

MONNIER
Bring the stools and pennants to the entrance on the
right. Hurry! Alfred, my boy, go, go ring the bell to
announce the end of the intermission! Alonzo,
quickly set up those flags by the barrier!

Sherlock leaves with the other riders and clowns.

MONNIER
(to Lupin)
Your Excellency, quick, return to your seat, the
second half is going to begin and I don't want you to
miss my pantomime.

LUPIN
(distracted)
Yes, of course.

MONNIER
It's not because I'm the author, you understand, but
because I think it's really good.

LUPIN
I don't doubt it for a minute.

MONNIER
It's called *The Bandits of Herzegovina.*

LUPIN
Ah, very good! Very good!

MONNIER
The Herzegovinan Hussars arrive at an inn on the side of a road on the edge of a forest. They drink and then they leave. A group of peasants, men and women, arrive and start to dance. Then they go. Then, brigands arrive and sack the inn. Suddenly, we hear bells. The brigands hide and a carriage arrives, carrying Magyar Petrousli–Nazir Pasha is interpreting the role which is full of whimsy.

LUPIN
Ah? So Nazir plays the Magyar?

MONNIER
I see you're already drawn to my story.

LUPIN
Enormously. Please continue, my dear Monnier. What happens next?

MONNIER
Well, the bandits then attack the carriage. The unfortunate Magyar is about to succumb when the Hussars return. There is a big battle with plenty of rifle shots. The brigands are cut to pieces and the Magyar leaves after having thanked his rescuers. It's original, isn't it?

LUPIN
You've whetted my appetite. I'm returning to my seat at once so as not to lose a minute of that spectacle.

MONNIER

Go, Prince, go!

Ganimard returns. Monnier notices him at once.

MONNIER

Good Lord, who's this strange-looking character?
I've never seen him around before.

LUPIN
(improvising)
He's a friend from my Club. I've brought him here
because he'd like to be a performer, but he's very
shy. He'd like to make his debut incognito.

MONNIER

I'd be delighted to be of service, Prince. You know,
he's perfect. He'd be just right as a clown...

Monnier leaves. Lupin looks at Ganimard, an idea taking
shape in his mind.

LUPIN
(aside)
I think I've just found the way to save Maud from
this idiot...

He walks to Ganimard.

LUPIN

My dear Chief Inspector, I have a very grave matter
to impart to you.

GANIMARD

To me?

LUPIN

You know what admiration I have for your incomparable genius.

GANIMARD
(modestly)
Ah, Prince! You're exaggerating!

LUPIN

Not at all! Not at all! You're the greatest detective in the world. One of the glories of our country. I can't bear the thought that an Englishman like that Sherlock has come here to ridicule you.

GANIMARD

What do you mean, ridicule me?

LUPIN

A sign I intercepted, whispers I overheard, all make me think I'm not mistaken. Lupin is here. And if Sherlock Holmes asked you to arrest Miss Clark, it's only because he wants the glory of arresting Lupin himself while you're busy elsewhere.

GANIMARD

I see. If only I could beat him to the punch... But how to find Lupin? He's a master of disguise. How to recognize him?

LUPIN

As it happens, I've just learned that he's going to play the part of the Magyar in the pantomime.

GANIMARD

And a Russian to boot! I'm going to cuff him right away!

LUPIN

That's right, my friend. Go quickly and good luck!

GANIMARD

Don't worry. I won't let him escape again.

He leaves.

LUPIN

(alone)
That Ganimard is incomparable.

Fouinard rushes in.

FOUINARD

Boss! Boss!

LUPIN

What is it?

FOUINARD

(very frightened)
There's a whole slew of policemen in the tent and they posted gendarmes at every door.

LUPIN

(very calm)
I know.

FOUINARD

We've got to get out of here, quick!

LUPIN

Not yet! Listen. You're going to leave right away and wait for me at my villa in Passy. I'll be there in an hour with Miss Clark.

FOUINARD
Fine, boss. Is that all?

LUPIN
That's all. The rest is Ganimard's concern. Come!

They leave.

After a moment, Sherlock Holmes enters, still disguised as a circus rider. After looking around, he goes to a small barrel standing unobtrusively in a corner. He knocks on it; the top comes up and Frederick appears, dressed as a small clown.

HOLMES
Well?

FREDERICK
Ganimard told him everything.

HOLMES
(joyous)
I knew he would. What happened after that?

FREDERICK
He said that in an hour he'll be with Miss Clark in his villa in Passy.

HOLMES
In his villa in Passy. All right! This time, Frederick, I guarantee you that we've got Lupin and the diamond.

Suddenly, we hear noise in the wings. Holmes gets Frederick back inside the barrel, closes the lid behind and pretends to busy himself. Ganimard enters, followed by policemen dragging Nazir despite his resistance. Everyone from the circus, including Monnier, is following them, protesting loudly.

NAZIR

I protest! I protest! I'm not Arsène Lupin! I am Nazir Pasha.

GANIMARD

(to his men)
Go! Go! To the prison. And give it to him!

The policemen pummel Nazir and drag him out. Nazir, Ganimard and the cops leave, except for two men who turn back and bar the door to the circus personnel who come on stage.

MONNIER

(in despair)
This is frightful! This is horrible! My beautiful pantomime in ruined.

FEMALE CLOWN

Perhaps, we could cut out the part.

MONNIER

(delighted)
Good Lord! What a superb idea. Come, my children. A little editing and in five minutes, we'll ring the bell.

CURTAIN

Scene XII

The Ring of Circus Monnier

The stage represents the Ring of Circus Monnier. Three-quarters are surrounded by boxes and benches, all occupied by an elegant audience. The last quarter is a stage, whose curtain is lowered.

At the beginning of the scene, a circus rider has just completed his number. He's applauded. The horseman salutes as a groom leads the horse off. Then, he, too, leaves. A gong strikes. It is now time for the pantomime *The Bandits of Herzegovina*.

The curtain rises on a view of the Balkan countryside. The innkeeper appears at the door of his inn, to the right. He calls his wife and they begin to welcome their customers, local farmers of both sexes. A trumpet call announces the arrival of the Hussars, who enter from the back. The innkeeper serves them drinks. Then, they leave.

Suddenly the brigands emerge–the farmers flee in terror. The bandits start to sack the inn, but the Hussars return. They pursue the bandits, who leave their loot behind and run away. The farmers come back–the local women thank the Hussars for their intervention with a final dance.

CURTAIN

Scene XIII

Arsène Lupin's villa in Passy

The décor is that of an ordinary elegant interior where nothing looks even remotely suspicious. Fouinard is stretched out in an armchair, sleeping. The stage is almost dark. A clock outside strikes 2 p.m.

FOUINARD

(yawning)

Two in the afternoon. And the boss has not yet arrived. Screw it, I'm going to go back to sleep. Goodnight, ladies and gentlemen–

Suddenly, one hears an auto horn outside. Fouinard gets up and goes to the window.

FOUINARD

It's the boss with the American chick. Let's mind our manners.

He leaves. A few seconds later, he returns, accompanied by Lupin, dressed as Prince Mirand, and Maud.

LUPIN

Tell the chauffeur to come and wait for me here.

FOUINARD

Right, boss, er, Your Excellency.

He withdraws.

MAUD

Prince Mirand, when you brought me here, you told
me that André was in great danger. Where is he? I
want to see him. To speak to him.

Lupin goes to the window, which he opens.

LUPIN

Rest assured, Mademoiselle, that André will know
enough not to be late. I just sent someone to tell him
of our arrival.

MAUD

I'm in a hurry to learn what danger threatens him,
since you have refused to tell me anything.

LUPIN

I prefer to leave that task to Monsieur Largery himself. Will you be kind enough to wait for him in this
drawing room next door? It's rather late and I'd like
to ask your permission to retire.

MAUD

Of course, Prince. I'll see you later.

LUPIN
(kissing her hand)
Until later then.

Maud leaves and Lupin shuts the door behind her. He then
reflects for a moment.

LUPIN

Now, I must find a way of convincing her to leave
with me. She must do it!

Lupin leaves by another door. There is a short pause. Then Fouinard returns, this time followed by Sherlock Holmes, disguised as a chauffeur wearing goggles.

FOUINARD
Wait here. His Excellency wants to speak with you.

HOLMES
That's all right.

Fouinard leaves, but returns from time to time to look suspiciously at Holmes.

HOLMES
(aside)
What can this rascal want? Could he be suspecting me? No, it's impossible! He can't suspect anything. Let's take a quick glance around here...

Holmes takes off his goggles and walks about the room, testing the furniture, the woodwork and the tapestry.

HOLMES
All very ordinary. Simple furniture.
(examining an armchair)
With a certain honest, bourgeois quality.
(noticing an armor)
Ha, what do we have here?
(examining it and striking it)
No, it attracts too much attention. He wouldn't be naïve enough to hide the diamond here...

He turns to the other side of the room.

HOLMES
Let's have a bit of a look over here...

He walks past an armoire, then backtracks and stops to take a closer look at it.

> HOLMES
> Wait, did I hear someone in there?
> (he listens closely)
> No, nothing. Still, I'm sure I heard–
> (he notices the armoire is
> slightly ajar)
> Hm. I don't care for armoires that aren't locked, especially when they may be occupied... Let's secure my means of escape.

He walks back to the door by which he came and tries to open it, but it resists.

> HOLMES
> Locked! Fine! What about the window.

He goes to the window, opens the window and sees that it is barred.

> HOLMES
> I suspected as much. Here we go. I'm trapped again. But even if I can't get out of here–there are other ways–

Holmes tears a page from his small notebook and starts writing.

> HOLMES
> "Frederick, go this instant to tell the police to come and surround the 15 rue Mozart in Passy where Lupin is to be found."

He folds the paper.

HOLMES
There's the message. Now to find the courrier.

He pulls out a little fox terrier from the pocket of his great coat, attaches the note to the dog and carries it to the window.

HOLMES
Toby! Find Frederick! Frederick. You understand? Go! Go!

He releases the dog, which jumps through the window.

HOLMES
All right! There's the perfect postman–never on strike.

He closes the window. Then, he hears the door bolt grind open, and puts his goggles back on. Lupin (dressed as Prince Mirand) enters.

LUPIN
I just found out that you've been kind enough to replace my chauffeur who found himself suddenly ill. All that trouble deserves a reward. Will you accept this?

He opens a jewel box and shows it to Holmes.

HOLMES
The Sultan Diamond!

LUPIN
Beautiful, isn't it, my dear Mister Holmes?

HOLMES
(looking him in the eyes)
Much, my dear Monsieur Lupin.

They discard their respective disguises.

> LUPIN
>
> It has to be said–you're indeed a worthy adversary. It certainly mustn't have been easy for you to leave my underground lair. Unfortunately, you've wasted your advantage...
>> (pointing to the door by which
>> he just came in)
>
> Go in there. Right now.

Holmes points to the other door, by which he himself came in.

> HOLMES
>
> I'd rather leave through that door, if you don't mind. And with the Sultan Diamond.

> LUPIN
>
> Very funny! Unfortunately, I'm in a hurry and not in a mood to laugh. Go in there, or else–
>> (making a threatening gesture)

> HOLMES
>> (mockingly)
>
> Or else?

Lupin rings a bell on the table. The doors of the armoire open and two men leap on Holmes–but at the last minute, he pulls a revolver and aims at them.

> HOLMES
>
> Hands up!
>> (noticing Lupin about to jump on him)
>
> Ah–you, too!

Holmes now aims at Lupin. To cover both the Gentleman Burglar and his two men, he is forced to step back, and by so doing, gets close to the suit of armor.

The armor suddenly springs to life, raises its arms and grabs Holmes by the shoulders, immobilizing him. The Detective fires–but misses. The two men disarm him. The revolver falls on the ground during the struggle.

Lupin points to the armoire.

LUPIN

Put him in there and be quick about it.

The two men thrust Holmes through the middle door. Then, at a gesture from Lupin, they leave by the side doors from which they came. Lupin notices the revolver and picks it up.

Suddenly, Maud enters, looking very upset. She runs towards him.

MAUD

André! André!

Lupin takes her hands in his.

LUPIN

Maud! My dearest Maud, what's the matter?

MAUD

Those shouts. That shot.

LUPIN

Calm down. It's nothing. I merely touched the trigger and it went off by accident. I assure you, no one's hurt. Look. I'm alone. All alone.

MAUD

Prince Mirand told me that you were in great danger.

LUPIN

He exaggerated. Probably because he knew how sad
I would have been to leave without having seen you
again–

MAUD
(stupefied)
You're about to leave?

LUPIN

Yes, in a few hours.

MAUD

Why didn't you tell me of your departure?

LUPIN

Because, even yesterday, I was still unaware of it.

MAUD

Will you be absent for a long time?

LUPIN

I'm leaving forever.

MAUD

Forever? Why? What does it all mean? The Prince's
mysterious words convinced me to come here. Then,
there's this gunshot, those shouts I'm quite certain I
heard–and now, your sudden departure... This is insane. Please, tell me what's going on.

LUPIN
(with effort)
I can't.

MAUD

I've got a right to know. You must tell me.

LUPIN

Maud, I love you more than the whole world! Ask for
my life, it's yours. But this secret isn't mine. I have
sworn to keep it forever–and I cannot break my oath.
Goodbye, Maud. Goodbye–forever!

Lupin rushes to the door.

MAUD

(letting out a scream)

André!

Lupin stops abruptly.

MAUD

I won't ask you any more questions–for I'm sure that
you are the most honest of men. But, before you
leave, I have a last request...

LUPIN

A request?

MAUD

Yes! Will you let me come with you?

LUPIN

(very moved)

Maud! What do you mean? You would consent to–?

MAUD

Shouldn't a wife follow her husband?

LUPIN

My wife! You! Oh, Maud! Maud! How I love you!

Lupin kisses Maud's face. At the same moment, a whistle
blow is heard in the street below. Lupin shivers.

MAUD
(surprised)
What's wrong, André?

LUPIN
(staggering)
Wrong? Nothing! Nothing!

There is a second whistle.

MAUD
(upset)
Yes. You've become quite pale and trembling. Oh,
my God, I understand. It's that danger that threatens
you, isn't it? The whistle blow–it's a signal! But I'll
protect you! They'll have to kill me before getting to
you. Speak! Say something, André!

LUPIN
(with style)
My name's not André, Maud. I am Arsène Lupin, the
Gentleman Burglar.

MAUD
(terrified)
You're Arsène Lupin? You?

LUPIN

Yes.

Maud bursts into tears and falls into a chair.

MAUD

Oh My God! My God!

LUPIN

I understand! It's a horrible thing! That a bandit of my sort may have pretended to your hand... What aberration! But, it was stronger than me. I loved you so much. I had a crazy dream. I wanted to take you far, far away–where no one would have known my past. We would have been happy! Alas, that police whistle has just awakened me to terrible reality. I now understand the unworthiness of my conduct. But I've confessed my real identity to you, I swear I'll redeem myself–make amends for my past. Will you forgive me, Maud?

Maud remains silent.

LUPIN
(in anguish)

Please!

Maud still says nothing. There is a long pause. Lupin is overwhelmed and rushes madly to the door.

LUPIN

Well, then, all that remains for me to do is to settle my accounts with the law... Goodbye, Maud!

MAUD
(nearly hysterical)

Stop!

LUPIN

What did you say?

MAUD

I said–I said–I want to know that it's not because of me that you're going to give yourself up.

LUPIN

Why would I do that, if it wasn't for you? Don't you think that I have a dozen ways of fleeing this place? But, since you hate me–I might as well end it now...

He turns back to the door.

MAUD
(struggling with herself)
No, no–it's impossible! I don't want it!

LUPIN

Then, you agree to forgive me?

MAUD
(finally)
Yes. I will forgive you. But only if you become an honest man again.

LUPIN

I swear to you that I will become worthy of you.

He retreats to the fireplace and presses an invisible button. The fireplace moves like a drawbridge and reveals a staircase hidden inside the depths of the wall.

Lupin goes up the steps; at the top, he turns and shouts:

LUPIN
'Till we meet again, Maud. *Au revoir*!

Lupin disappears. The fireplace has barely moved back into its previous location than an uproar of voices is heard. The left side door is forced open and Ganimard appears abruptly, followed by a squad of policemen.

GANIMARD
(noticing Maud)
Where is the wretch? Where is he?

MAUD
(calmly)
Who are you? What do you want?

GANIMARD
Where is Arsène Lupin?

MAUD
Arsène Lupin?
(regaining her self-control)
Why, I don't know, Monsieur. I don't understand
what you mean.

GANIMARD
You can't fool an old fox like me, Mademoiselle!
I know that Arsène Lupin is here.
(pointing to a paper)
Here's a letter which leaves me in no doubt on that
matter.

MAUD
I'm telling you again, Monsieur–I don't understand
what you mean.

GANIMARD
Fine, fine, Mademoiselle. I know what I've got to do.
(to his men)
Search the house!

ALL
At once, Chief Inspector.

They begin ransacking the place.

GANIMARD
As for you, Mademoiselle, since you continue to
pretend that Arsène Lupin isn't here–then, it must
mean that you're his accomplice. Therefore, I've got
no choice but to place you under arrest.

MAUD
Me?!

GANIMARD
Yes, you!

Frederick enters, with Toby on a leash.

FREDERICK
And you're about to make another mistake, Chief
Inspector.

GANIMARD
Say, you little brat, you're not going to teach me my
job, I suppose.

FREDERICK
Oh, that wouldn't be too difficult.

At this moment, there is a loud noise coming from the armoire. Its doors spring open and Sherlock Holmes appears in a
cloud of smoke. Maud utters a terrified scream.

HOLMES

Frederick is right, Monsieur Ganimard. Madame is
not Lupin's accomplice, but rather, his victim, for he
lured her here to rob her.

GANIMARD

How do you know that?

HOLMES

I was locked in this armoire from where I heard
everything. As I didn't have the key, I blew off its
bolt with a little explosive cartridge.

FREDERICK

Oh–very ingenious! Good evening, Papa.

HOLMES

(going to Maud, bowing)
Mademoiselle, you are free.

MAUD

Thank you, Monsieur.

Maud leaves, saluted by Sherlock and Frederick.

GANIMARD

All this is very sweet. But I came here to arrest Lupin
and I won't leave before having done it.

HOLMES

Alas, my dear Chief Inspector, you can no longer
count on doing that–at least, tonight.

GANIMARD

Why's that?

HOLMES
Because he's already left!

GANIMARD
Impossible! The house is surrounded by my men.

HOLMES
Do you think that would prevent him from escaping?
Do you only know how he escaped?

GANIMARD
No.

HOLMES
Through this fireplace.

GANIMARD
You're pulling my leg!

HOLMES
I wouldn't dream of such familiarity. Would you like
to bet on it, say, five francs?

GANIMARD
(pointing to the fireplace)
That he escaped through there?

HOLMES
Yes.

GANIMARD
Yes, I would. You're on, by Jove!

FREDERICK
Would you also bet five francs with me, Chief Inspector?

GANIMARD

Now you're talking, brat.

FREDERICK

All right!

GANIMARD
(mockingly)
Well, I'm waiting for you to show me how he did it.

Holmes looks for, and eventually finds, the hidden spring. He releases it.

HOLMES

Like this!

The fireplace moves.

GANIMARD

Well, I'll be...!

Holmes holds out his hand.

HOLMES
The five francs, if you please.

Frederick also holds out his hand.

FREDERICK
And me too, if you please.

Ganimard pulls out his wallet and pays them.

GANIMARD
(sourly)
Well, this isn't what I came here for.

FREDERICK
(sarcastic)
Really, you'd have been better off staying home.

CURTAIN

Scene XIV

A very impressive room at Gottlieb's

AT RISE, we find most of the characters whom we already saw at the Pré-Catalan in Scene I. Everybody is talking as they take tea. It is 5 p.m.

Rebecca, dressed in a ridiculously elegant dress, offers a cup of tea to Madame des Epouffettes, seated on a sofa.

REBECCA
A cup of tea, Countess?

MME. DES EPOUFFETTES
Gladly, Mademoiselle.

REBECCA
You know, it's first-class tea.

MME. DES EPOUFFETTES
I have no doubt of that.

REBECCA
At my five o'clocks, I only serve the best quality products. The tea comes from the best house in Paris. Solomon forbids me from going anywhere else.

She turns to another guest, seated on the side.

REBECCA
A little dry cake, Miss Moore?

MISS MOORE
No, thank you.

189

REBECCA
Oh, please, do take one. They're not dry because they're old, they were made that way.

MME. DES EPOUFFETTES
I have no trouble believing you.
(aside to Miss Moore as
Rebecca moves away)
Well, do you think this is worth the trouble of being seen?

MISS MOORE
It's screamingly funny.

Solomon Gottlieb has been talking with a group of ladies and finishes the tale he's been telling.

GOTTLIEB
Yes, Mesdames and Messieurs, it's just as I told you. Last night, during the performance at Circus Monnier, Chief Inspector Ganimard arrested Nazir Pasha and took him back to the Sûreté, thinking he was Arsène Lupin! Nazir spent the night there and it was only this morning that they admitted they had made a mistake.

SAINT-GATIEN
(laughing)
Well—now that's what I call an adventure!

Everybody laughs.

GOTTLIEB
(laughing)
And when I went to have lunch at the Sûreté, I found poor Nazir completely depressed. There and then,

GOTTLIEB (cont'd)

I decided that what he needed was some peace and
quiet to recover from his emotions, so I took him to a
rest home I know. He'll stay there for a month but I'll
have my commissions within the week.

SAINT-GATIEN
(astonished)

Your commissions? I don't understand.

GOTTLIEB
(stuttering)

Er, I meant, a good month of rest will do him a great
deal of good.
(aside)

And me, too!

Suddenly, Nazir enters, red-faced and obviously upset.

NAZIR

By the beard of the Prophet!

GOTTLIEB
(aside)

Damn!

Rebecca runs to Nazir.

REBECCA

Nazir, my little Nazir!

NAZIR

Ah, you–stay away from me!

REBECCA
(scandalized)

Oh!

NAZIR
(to Gottlieb)
Can you tell me, Monsieur, why you took advantage
of my momentary depression to have me taken to a
rest home?

GOTTLIEB
Well, er, because–

NAZIR
No excuses. You had me sequestered so that you
could appropriate the Sultan Diamond!

ALL
(scandalized)
Oh!

GOTTLIEB
(laughing nervously)
Why, that's false! Absolutely false!

NAZIR
Then, return the diamond to me.

He holds out his hand.

GOTTLIEB
(defeated)
Ah, My God! My God! I'm afraid I don't have it
anymore, my dear Nazir.

ALL
Oh!

GOTTLIEB
Arsène Lupin stole it from me.

NAZIR

(laughing)
Arsène Lupin? Really? Ah! That's a good one–if I believed it!

GOTTLIEB

I swear it's the truth!

NAZIR

(violently)
Enough! I don't believe you! You're a cheat. But, by the beard of Mohammed, we'll see who has the last laugh, you swine!

He goes to the door. Rebecca runs towards him.

REBECCA

Nazir! My sweet little Nazir!

NAZIR

Ah, you, shut up. I don't want to hear a word from you. Tail of a comet! Ha!

They leave together.

GOTTLIEB

(overwhelmed)
I'm finished.

MME. DES EPOUFFETTES

This is abominable! I won't remain another minute in this house.

MISS MOORE

Nor I!

LORMELLES
(to Gottlieb)
You're a clown.

ROSEROY
A scoundrel.

SAINT-GATIEN
A thief!

MME. DES EPOUFFETTES
A usurer! A crocodile!

Gottlieb becomes terrified as they all raise and shake their canes, umbrellas and ladies' purses at him.

GOTTLIEB
Ah, My God! My God!

Suddenly, there is a booming voice.

VOICE
Stop!

Everybody stops and turns. Lupin, dressed and made up to look like Sherlock Holmes, enters.

LUPIN
Stop! You're all making a dreadful mistake.
Monsieur Gottlieb is right, he's innocent! It was, in-deed, Arsène Lupin who stole the Sultan Diamond.

ALL
(astonished)
Ah?

LORMELLES
Who are you, then, Monsieur?

LUPIN
I am Sherlock Holmes, consulting detective.

ALL
(with astonishment and admiration)
Sherlock Holmes!

LUPIN
In person! I found myself in Paris four days ago
when the theft of the Sultan Diamond occurred. The
case seemed interesting, so I resolved to solve it.

GOTTLIEB
(very moved)
Thank you, God!

LUPIN
I recently unmasked Lupin and recovered the diamond.

ALL
Ah!

GOTTLIEB
(delighted)
Ah, Mister Holmes. How can I express my gratitude?
Let me give you a reward...
(fumbling in his pocket)
I have only ten francs on me, but I will double the
sum later.

LUPIN

That won't be enough, Monsieur Gottlieb. If you want to get the diamond back, it'll cost you 100,000 francs.

GOTTLIEB

100,000 francs. Why?

LUPIN

To pay off Arsène Lupin! It's the price he demands to return the diamond.

GOTTLIEB
(furious)

100,000 francs! We must arrest this scoundrel! Take him to jail! Search him!

LUPIN

Nothing more simple, if that is your wish. I can have him under lock and key in five minutes. However, if I do this, the Sultan will forever be lost. Lupin entrusted it to an accomplice, whom he instructed to go and throw the stone into the sea if he is arrested.

GOTTLIEB
(desperate)

That's awful! That's terrible! What to do?

LUPIN

My advice is to pay him. That will cost you much less than reimbursing Nazir Pasha. After all, the Sultan is worth nearly 30 millions.

GOTTLIEB
(overwhelmed)

True, true! My God! Well, since there's no other way, I'll pay...

He pulls a checkbook from his pocket and writes a check. He signs it and gives it to Lupin.

> GOTTLIEB
> There you are. Poor me!

> LUPIN
> (looking at the check)
> It's perfectly in order.

He goes to Madame des Epouffettes.

> LUPIN
> Excuse me, Countess. I believe you are the President of the Paris chapter of the Red Cross?

> MME. DES EPOUFFETTES
> Why, yes, Monsieur.

> LUPIN
> Please, allow me to hand you this check.

> MME. DES EPOUFFETTES
> (astonished)
> To me? Why? I don't understand!

> LUPIN
> Arsène Lupin, having learned that Monsieur Gottlieb had omitted to contribute to this worthy institution, wanted to repair this involuntary oversight on his behalf. Monsieur Gottlieb, in ten minutes, I will have your diamond.

He heads towards the door. Suddenly, an Old Gentleman (the real Sherlock Holmes in disguise) who, until then, had remained in the background, rises and goes to him. He pretends to walk and speak with difficulty.

HOLMES
Pardon me, Monsieur, but if it isn't too indiscreet,
I would like to ask you a question...

LUPIN
Which one, Monsieur?

HOLMES
Are you really Sherlock Holmes?

LUPIN
Why, yes, of course.

HOLMES
Really?

LUPIN
Really!

HOLMES
The cheek! The infernal cheek! That's extremely
disturbing!

LUPIN
Why is that?

HOLMES
Because, if you are Sherlock Holmes, then I no
longer am who I am.

LUPIN
You mean?

HOLMES
I mean that I'm no longer who I am, since I, too, am
Sherlock Holmes!

He removes his disguise. There is a general uproar.

> GOTTLIEB
> What does this mean?

> LUPIN
> (daringly)
> It means that the gentleman is right. He really *is*
> Sherlock Holmes.

> GOTTLIEB
> Who, then, are you?

> LUPIN
> You'd really like to know?

> ALL
> Yes, indeed.

> LUPIN
> (removing his mask)
> Then, so be it. I am Arsène Lupin.

Everyone panics; some hide behind the furniture, screaming.

> LUPIN
> (breaking into laughter)
> Curtain!
> (to Sherlock)
> My compliments. It's five minutes to six. I'm beaten.
> Arrest me.

> HOLMES
> (with great dignity)
> I would have arrested Arsène Lupin gladly and with-
> out hesitation, but I've learned since that he is

199

HOLMES (cont'd)

leaving, never to return, forsaking his evil ways. He has asked one of his friends, André Largery, to help him repair the damages he's done. So there's no account to settle. You're free to go.

LUPIN

Thank you, Mister Holmes. You're an honorable adversary. Here's your diamond, Monsieur Gottlieb.

He deposits the stone on the table and is about to leave, when Ganimard enters, followed by Folenfant and Dieuzy.

GANIMARD

Don't anybody move! I've come at the request of Nazir Pasha to arrest Solomon Gottlieb.

He finds himself face-to-face with Lupin.

GANIMARD

Lupin!

LUPIN
(smiling)
What? That surprises you?

GANIMARD

Folenfant! Dieuzy! Grab him!

The two policemen grab Lupin.

GANIMARD

Finally! I've got you at last.

LUPIN
(after having looked about)
It looks like it, yes. And it wasn't so easy, was it?

GANIMARD

Cuff him!

LUPIN

Cuff *me*? You must be joking!

He pushes the two policemen and they fall down like pins.

LUPIN

No need for cuffs. If I go with you, it's because
I wish to, not because of your toys.

GANIMARD

OK! OK! Let's go, then! To the Sûreté!

LUPIN

The Sûreté! Oh, I wouldn't expect to stay there more
than a day.

GANIMARD

Why?

LUPIN

Because the folks there are not well brought up.

GANIMARD

Pah!

LUPIN
(to Holmes)
See you soon, my dear Mister Holmes.
(to the police)
Come on, flunkeys!

CURTAIN

Scene XV

The Great Hall at the Gare du Nord

At the back are trains on tracks, ready to depart. Only one track is free. In the distance, we see signal lights and several flags. As the curtain rises, a train enters the station. Uproar of travelers.

GANIMARD
(shouting very loudly)
Are you telling me, Stationmaster, that no special arrangements have been made and the Minister's special train is arriving in 10 minutes?

STATIONMASTER
But, Chief Inspector, the police and the workers are all here. They're only waiting for you to issue orders.

GANIMARD
I see. Me again, naturally. Always me. I've got to do everything here. Ah, Napoleon was lucky, being only an Emperor. I'd like to see him be Chief Inspector for an hour. C'mon, c'mon, hurry, hurry!

They leave, just as Solomon Gottlieb and Nazir Pasha enter, the latter dressed in traveling attire. They hold each other by the arm with an air of familiarity.

GOTTLIEB
So, my dear friend, you're forced to return to Mesopotamia?

NAZIR

Yes, we're having a bit of trouble. The junior branch of our government has just poisoned the senior.

GOTTLIEB

That's terrible!

NAZIR

Not really. We're used to it. It happens about every two years.

GOTTLIEB

Don't forget to send me my commissions and my titles.

NAZIR

Don't worry. Now that we are reconciled.

At this moment, Rebecca appears. She is followed by four porters, laboring under the weight of her heavy trunks. She's wearing a comical traveling attire.

REBECCA
(to the porters)
Pay attention! That's fragile. All of it.
(seeing Nazir)
Nazir–my little Nazir. You, at last.

NAZIR

Her! Again!

REBECCA

I only found out last night that you were going home and my blood froze in my veins. I immediately packed a few essentials and here I am! I'm going with you.

GOTTLIEB

Please, Rebecca, you must go home and not pester
our good friend Nazir anymore. For your own good.

REBECCA

(distraught)
But I love him! Nazir, my little Nazir–is it true that
you don't want me to go with you?

NAZIR

(with heart)
So much persistence and love deserves a reward.
Come, my pretty! In my arms, daughter of
Mohammed! I've booked a sleeping car just for the
two of us.

REBECCA

Ah, joy! Happiness! I knew that day would come!
I am a new woman!
(to the porters)
Pay attention to my hat boxes, you clumsy oafs!

They leave. Ganimard reappears at the head of his men (led by
Folenfant and Dieuzy) and the station workers.

GANIMARD

Line up in double file. And don't let anyone go
through. Whew! I'm hot.

Ganimard wipes his face. At this moment, Sherlock Holmes
arrives, dressed in travel clothes, with Frederick, dressed just
like him, and Toby.

HOLMES

(loudly)
I beg your pardon, but I'd really like to cross.

GANIMARD

Huh? What? What's the matter?
(recognizing Sherlock)
Oh, for goodness' sake. This is Mister Sherlock
Holmes. Let him pass.
(to Holmes)
How are you, my dear colleague?

HOLMES

As you see!

GANIMARD

You are going back to England?

HOLMES
(ironic)
You're as sharp as ever, Chief Inspector. Yes, I'm
going home with Frederick. He earned his spurs.
Now he's a real detective.

FREDERICK

I'm dressed like Papa, too.

GANIMARD
(strutting)
My compliments, young man. What a braggart that
Lupin was. He said he wouldn't stay in jail over a
day, and it has been 23 hours and he's still there.

HOLMES

Well, frankly, that surprises me a little.

FREDERICK

Me a lot, and Toby enormously.

There is the sound of a horn.

GANIMARD
Attention–here's the Minister! Men, present arms!

All the policemen and workers stand at attention. Lupin (for it
is he, of course!) enters, disguised as the Minister. He is escorted by the Stationmaster and three or four reporters. Ganimard steps forward.

GANIMARD
If the Minister would allow me, I'll escort him to his
private car. I'm Ganimard, Chief Inspector of the
Sûreté–the man who arrested Arsène Lupin.

LUPIN
Ah yes, I'm well aware of your heroic actions, Mon-
sieur Ganimard. In the name of the Republic of
France, I'm pleased to give you this medal.

He pulls out a huge medal and prepares to pin it on Ganimard's chest.

GANIMARD
(beaming)
Thank you, Minister. I wasn't expecting–
(he looks at the medal and
reacts in surprise)
–the Order of the Hay? Why, Minister, this is for
services rendered in Agriculture. It must be a mistake.

LUPIN
Possibly, possibly. It's a very popular medal, you
know? And when they spoke of you in government
circles, they mentioned the words "hayseed" so it
seemed appropriate.

GANIMARD
(naively)
I see.

The "Minister" is about to take the medal back but Ganimard stops him.

GANIMARD
Well, since you've got it with you, you might as well give it to me.

Lupin pins it on him, purposefully stabbing him with it. Ganimard grimaces and rubs his chest.

LUPIN
(to the crowd)
Being able to appropriately reward merit like that, gentlemen, is the one good thing about being in power.
(noticing Holmes)
Why, if I'm not mistaken, this is Mister Sherlock Holmes?

HOLMES
You recognize me, Minister?

LUPIN
By reputation only. I've heard of your many exploits, of course.

HOLMES
The Minister is too kind.

LUPIN
(pointing to Fred)
And this young man is your son?

HOLMES

Yes, Minister.

LUPIN

He's charming! Allow me to embrace you, young man?

FREDERICK
(on tiptoe so the Minister can hug him)
I'd be honored, Minister.

LUPIN
(low)
Tell your father that Arsène Lupin wishes him *bon voyage*!

FREDERICK
(aloud)
I won't fail to–Minister.

LUPIN

Gentlemen, I salute you.

He goes toward the train. Many acclamations follow him. Somewhere, they play the *Marseillaise*! At this moment, a gentleman arrives, the real Minister of course, but he finds his way barred by Sergeant Folenfant.

MINISTER

Let me pass! Let me pass!

FOLENFANT

No! No way!

MINISTER

Oh, this is too much!

He tries to force his way through. They push him back. There is a violent altercation.

GANIMARD

What's this all about? You'd better shut your trap, you guttersnipe.

MINISTER
(furious)
You're the guttersnipe, you ugly ape.

GANIMARD

If you keep giving me lip, you're going to get a good drubbing.

The policemen pommel the Minister with their fists and truncheons. His hat is ruined. They give him a black eye. At this moment, the train starts moving amidst great acclamation from the crowd.

Suddenly, to everyone's stupefaction, a man standing on the last car (Fouinard) unrolls an enormous banner upon which is written: "*To Ganimard: goodbye and all my love, Arsène Lupin.*" Everyone bursts out laughing.

GANIMARD
(stupefied)
What kind of joke is that? What does it mean?

HOLMES
(enjoying himself)
It means, my dear Chief Inspector, that it was Lupin himself who just left in that train, passing himself off as your Minister.

GANIMARD
My God! Where's the real Minister then?

The real Minister, in rags, who had collapsed in the arms of the police, now gets up.

> MINISTER
>
> I'm right here! I'm the real Minister! And you're fired!

Ganimard collapses in the arms of the Stationmaster as Sherlock Holmes and Frederick double up laughing.

> CROWD
>
> Long live the Minister! Long live the Minister!

The *Marseillaise* starts up again. The Minister, trying to restore his ragged hat, bows and walks upstage.

> CURTAIN

The Real Sherlock Holmes

by

Frank J. Morlock

Characters

Sherlock Holmes
Dr. Watson
Irene Adler Norton
Professor James Moriarty
Mycroft Holmes

The scene is Baker Street. Everything is packed to leave. Chairs are covered with sheets. Only a few things of Holmes' remain. The Persian slipper where Holmes kept his tobacco and his pipe are on a table. Watson is pacing up and down meditatively.

> WATSON
>
> Enough of this sentimentality, it's time to go. There's no point in my staying here anymore. The associations are too painful.
> (picking up the pipe and slipper)
> Holmes is dead and no amount of grieving will bring him back to life. Memories! To think I used to be annoyed that he kept his tobacco in a slipper. What I would give to see him alive and well again!

He replaces the slipper. There is a knock at the door.

> WATSON
>
> Well, well...

He goes to open the door.

> WATSON
>
> That must be Mrs. Hudson or the cabby.

He opens the door.

> WATSON
>
> Irene Adler!

Irene Adler enters. She is a regally-dressed woman of great beauty.

> IRENE
>
> Dr. Watson! I didn't expect to see you here.

WATSON
Well, this is a pleasant surprise.

IRENE
You look as though you are leaving.

WATSON
I'm taking new lodgings. But what are you doing in
London? I thought you had gone to Paris?

IRENE
I'm returning to the stage. I'm singing Marguerite
in *Faust*.

WATSON
Indeed. I should be glad to hear you sing. I have often
regretted that I never had the pleasure.

IRENE
Thank you so much, Dr. Watson. You were always
very gallant.

WATSON
Not at all! I meant it sincerely.

IRENE
It's your sincerity that makes you so gallant, you see.

WATSON
Have you been well, I trust, these last few years?

IRENE
(uneasily)
Oh, very well. I don't allow things to get me down.
(pointedly)
And, where is your companion, Mr. Holmes?

WATSON

Ah, you must not have known. The best of men is
dead–one year ago this month.

IRENE
(surprised)
Indeed, I didn't know. I hadn't heard from–of him
in some time.

WATSON

It is a loss which not only I, but the whole world must
suffer.

IRENE
(passionately)
Permit me to say: the world can manage very well
without Mr. Sherlock Holmes!

WATSON
I beg you to change your tone immediately.

IRENE
Your devotion is quite touching.

WATSON
Never mind my devotion.

IRENE
I am sorry to offend you, Dr. Watson, but despite
his intellect, which I admit was peerless, he was a
scoundrel!

WATSON
Really, Miss Adler, I cannot allow such a reflection
on his memory even from a lady for whom I entertain
the highest regard. And, may I add a lady that

WATSON (cont'd)
Sherlock Holmes honored above all others.

IRENE
Dr. Watson, your feelings do you great honor. But, unfortunately, I am certain of what I say.

WATSON
But, surely, Miss Adler, you can bear Holmes no grudge for trying to recover that photograph of you and a certain royal personage–in order to prevent what must be admitted was a form of blackmail–even though your motive in threatening to expose His Majesty was jealousy, not venality. You can hardly complain of the ruse he employed. Besides, you yourself, actually bested him. And finally, it was of your own free will that you destroyed the photograph when you married Alfred Norton!

IRENE
Oh, on that score, I bear him no ill will. It was fair play. It was for the other things he did to me.

WATSON
(cheerfully)
Well, then, you see there is no basis for rancor–

IRENE
The rancor is for the years he blackmailed me after that–

WATSON
(astounded)
Blackmailed you! What are you talking about?

IRENE

Something you evidently know nothing about. If you did, you wouldn't bandy words with me!

WATSON

I'm completely at sea.

IRENE

It's hardly surprising. If I were Sherlock Holmes, I shouldn't tell an honorable man about it, either. Not if I hoped to retain his respect.

WATSON

I am certain there is some mistake which can easily be put right. I beg you to tell me the story.

IRENE

You will recall, Dr. Watson, that I willingly gave up the photograph and all hopes of revenge when I chose to marry Alfred Norton. It was the least I could do for a man who married me with full knowledge of all my prior indiscretions and who never once mentioned them to me. I hardly expected Sherlock Holmes to pursue me across the Continent and destroy my marriage. Yes, I fled him. But it was no use.

WATSON

What you are saying is incredible.

IRENE

Sherlock Holmes persecuted me for three years.

WATSON

I don't believe it.

IRENE

I will prove it. As you know, Dr. Watson, your friend
had the reputation of being indifferent to women.

WATSON

You were the only woman he ever found attractive.

IRENE

Who would suspect him of being a lecher?

WATSON

Frau Adler, this is too much! This is indecent!

IRENE

He ruined my marriage, Dr. Watson. When I left
London, I was supremely confident that I would live
happily with my husband. My husband was not
wealthy but he had an income of some sort. I had
turned my back on my past. And my past, as you
know, had included many men, even a prince or two.

WATSON

I read the file.

IRENE

I was in love with my husband. He was a wonderful
man, never jealous and perfectly indifferent to the
prejudices of this age about proper behavior for a
woman. In short, he was irresistible. He was proud of
me. I think nothing could have destroyed my marriage, except the malevolence of Sherlock Holmes.

WATSON

Holmes was never malevolent.

IRENE

You will judge for yourself. I was living a retired life
in Paris with my husband, when I received a communication from Sherlock Holmes that he must see me
on urgent business. I was a little surprised, but I had
such a good opinion of him that I agreed at once to
meet him.

WATSON

There, you admit–

IRENE

Hear me out! I walked blindly into the trap that he
had set for me. When we met, there was an unpleas-
ant glint in his eyes. He asked me if I remembered
Admiral Kovalevsky.

WATSON

I recall Holmes was interested in Kovalevsky. He
was murdered in Berlin and Holmes thought Moriarty
had something to do with it. But, you knew Kovalevsky?

IRENE

Yes. I had been his companion for several months
about five years previously.

WATSON

Undoubtedly Holmes sought your assistance in solv-
ing the murder.

IRENE

I thought that, too. I told him I didn't see how I could
help him, as I hadn't been in touch with the Admiral
in many years.

WATSON

I see.

IRENE

It was then he said that the Admiral's death was of no concern to me. However, the Admiral had died possessed of some photographs of me, which had come into your friend's possession.

WATSON

I am surprised that Holmes didn't simply destroy them.

IRENE

Your naivete is amazing, Dr. Watson. The Admiral had got me drunk on Vodka, and well, the photographs he took were not merely compromising, they were obscene. I speak as a woman who is not shy in such matters.

WATSON

Good Heavens!

IRENE

I didn't know the photographs existed until afterwards. The Admiral refused to part with them when he separated from me. He wanted them for his personal collection. He promised never to show them to anyone.

WATSON

Did he?

IRENE

Men like to boast, but I believe he never did. He never sought to blackmail me. In his funny Russian way, the Admiral was the soul of honor.

WATSON

But, why would Holmes–?

IRENE

I was stupid enough to think he wanted to return
them to me.

WATSON

And–

IRENE

He demanded–

WATSON

Money? I'll never believe it.

IRENE

Not money. Absolute obedience. I said "no." He then
passed me one of the photographs. I turned scarlet. I
never had blushed before in my life. No, not even
when the Duchess of Amalfi discovered me in bed
with her husband.

WATSON

Finish your story.

IRENE

I asked what I must do. He told me that I would
receive instructions.

WATSON

I know my protests make no impression, Frau Adler,
but this is inconceivable.

IRENE

No less to you than it was to me. But I had to obey. I
couldn't let my husband ever see such photographs.

WATSON
(cautiously)
What demands did he make?

IRENE

At first, simple ones. Hardly necessary to employ
threats. Meet him at this or that cafe wearing a
corsage or bracelet. Mere obedience training. Then,
suddenly he ordered me to meet him at Lake Como.
It was dreadful. I had no plausible excuse for going to
Italy, and I abhorred lying to my husband. I told him
to trust me. I kept the appointment.

WATSON

And what did you do there?

IRENE

At first, nothing. I was furious. Then I was ordered to
meet a Russian woman and accept a packet from her.
I did as instructed. A week later, the packet was
picked up by an English lady. I returned to Paris and
patched things up as well as I could with my
husband.

WATSON

This is all very bizarre.

IRENE

Nothing happened for several months. Then Holmes
appeared again and this time I had to go to Venice.
Immediately! I begged. I stormed. I offered to become his mistress. Holmes was implacable! I went.

IRENE (cont'd)
I had no conception of what horrors awaited me in
Venice. I expected another routine courier operation.

WATSON
And?

IRENE
More was expected of me. When I heard his vile arrangements, I nearly fainted.

WATSON
What did he want of you?

IRENE
His Majesty, the King of Bohemia (you know his real
title) was on a state visit. I was instructed to resume
my liaison with him.

WATSON
Surely, you refused?

IRENE
Outright! I pointed out that His Majesty and I had
parted on very unfriendly terms and that we were
both married. Holmes asked me how long my current
marriage would last if my husband received those
photographs. I still refused. Better exposure than this.

WATSON
Good for you! I am sure you would refuse such a
demand.

IRENE
But, my marriage was doomed anyway, as your
friend quickly pointed out to me.

WATSON

Why?

IRENE

Because as soon as my husband learned that the King of Bohemia was in Venice, he would never believe that I went there for any purpose but to renew the liaison. I laughed at Holmes then. I told him he had at least set me free.

WATSON

That was certainly the right thing to do.

IRENE

But, it was not to be. Holmes pointed out that I had been engaged in espionage under his direction for the last six months. He told me I could expect to spend the next ten years of my life in prison–if the courts were merciful.

WATSON

This is dastardly! Dastardly!

IRENE

The next day, by a cleverly arranged accident, I met His Majesty. To my surprise, he was delighted to see me.

WATSON

That hardly surprises me at all.

IRENE

Now that he was legally married, he cared nothing for the Princess' jealousy. He practically jumped for joy when he met me. He thought because he harbored no resentment towards me that I felt none towards him. What fools men are! Not only did I resent the

IRENE (cont'd)

way he had treated me in the past, I blamed him for
the destruction of my marriage. Oh, how I hated him.

WATSON

(musing)

That must have fallen in perfectly with Holmes'
plans–

IRENE

I didn't care. His Majesty is very weak, you know.
Easily managed. My instructions were to reduce him
to complete submission. Never have orders been
more willingly obeyed. It was so easy.

WATSON

This is horrible.

IRENE

My prolonged absence made it impossible to keep the
affair from my husband. He learned of it and committed suicide by throwing himself in the Seine. Do
you see why I hate Sherlock Holmes?

WATSON

Is it possible that I never really knew the man? That
he deceived me completely?

IRENE

He was a German or Austrian agent, Dr. Watson. He
had to be.

WATSON

Will you let me try to prove it is not so? I have my
records packed up here. If I can prove that Holmes
was in London or that he wasn't where you believe
him to have been?

IRENE

I am willing to listen. But, don't you see? The man led a double life. We'll never know who he really was.

WATSON

But, why did you come here?

IRENE

I came here to kill him.

WATSON

What!

IRENE

When I learned of my husband's death, I had a breakdown. I only recently recovered. I decided to revenge myself.

WATSON

You had a breakdown?

IRENE

Yes. I was beyond his power. I started crying. I cried all day for two years. His Majesty left me in a sanitarium. I must say, he was kind to me. He paid all my bills quite regularly. I didn't know that Holmes was dead, you see, or I wouldn't have come. Even in death, he has cheated me.
(giving her hand to Dr. Watson)
I'm going. It's just as well, I suppose. Come see me sing. They say I've gained a lot as a singer recently. Before I never could sing tragedy.

She goes out.

WATSON
(sitting down, bowing his head)
It can't be. It can't be.

CABBIE
(knocking and entering)
Ar' you the bloke what ordered a cab?

WATSON
What? Yes. How did you get in?

CABBIE
Door's wide open, mate. Say, are you all right? Look
like you had some kind of tragedy?

WATSON
No, no. I'll be myself presently. Just wait a bit.

Watson sits down.

HOLMES
Watson, my dear fellow, what's wrong?

WATSON
(staring at the Cabby)
Holmes, is it you?

HOLMES
None other. See.
(throwing off his disguise)
I am flesh and blood.

WATSON
But, how? By what miracle did you survive that fall
into the Reichenbach?

HOLMES

No miracle. I couldn't have survived it, if I had
fallen. I say, it was thoughtful of you to keep my pipe
and slipper.

        (goes to pipe and fills it)

Do you know the hardest thing about a disguise is the
inability to do simple things like enjoy a pipe?

WATSON

Holmes, in God's name, where have you been for the
last year?

HOLMES

All in good time, my dear fellow. Obviously, I didn't
fall.

WATSON

But, all the evidence!

HOLMES

It was a put-up job, Watson. I walked away as I had
come.

WATSON

And Moriarty?

HOLMES

We left together.

WATSON

What!

HOLMES

The deception I practiced on you was the most difficult thing I've ever had to do in my life. But it was
necessary the world think me dead. Especially you,
dear Watson.

WATSON

I don't understand at all. How was Moriarty involved in this?

HOLMES

We planned it together. A trifle melodramatic, but Moriarty's brain works that way, and he convinced me that nothing better would serve our turn.

WATSON

"Our turn," Holmes? But, Moriarty was the Arch-Enemy. What is going on? Explain yourself immediately.

HOLMES

It was necessary so that we, Moriarty and I, could undertake a secret mission for Her Majesty. I have just completed it.

WATSON

But, what had Moriarty to do with such a mission? Why was he meant to appear dead?

HOLMES

Moriarty needed his freedom, too. He could no longer continue his work in London. He was needed elsewhere.

WATSON

Holmes, I understand none of this. Are you suggesting Moriarty was also engaged in special service?

HOLMES

An explanation is in order.

WATSON

And long overdue.

HOLMES

Certain things I can tell you, but others I cannot reveal. Even to you, my dear friend. It began with the death of Admiral Kovalevsky in Berlin.

WATSON

Kovalevsky!

HOLMES

You recall I suspected Moriarty of being responsible for that murder?

WATSON

Yes, yes, I recall.

HOLMES

I was perfectly correct, of course. I had absolute proof and I confronted Moriarty.

WATSON

Then, for God's sake, man, why didn't you bring him to justice?

HOLMES

Because he had committed no crime.

WATSON

Stop talking in riddles, Holmes. Is murder no crime?

HOLMES

Picture me confronting Professor Moriarty at gunpoint–preparing to bring him to the gallows or kill him if he resisted arrest.

FLASHBACK. The stage darkens. Holmes and Moriarty are spotlighted.

HOLMES
Your criminal career is over, Professor. A great career, I would be the first to admit. But finished.

MORIARTY
What makes you think I am a criminal, Mr. Sherlock Holmes?

HOLMES
What else can one think of a man who had been behind every major criminal act in this and several other European capitals?

MORIARTY
But, is that not in itself suggestive?

HOLMES
Yes. Of megalomania. I've said many times you are the Napoleon of Crime.

MORIARTY
I prefer to think of myself as Caesar. But to what end? Criminals are no doubt very selfish individuals– but the megalomaniacs join the army, the civil service, or better yet become politicians. They aspire to rule the world, not the underworld.

HOLMES
As a general observation, undoubtedly true. Still, we have your example.

MORIARTY
Please observe that I do not deny that I am a megalomaniac.

HOLMES

Yes, you merely pointed out that a megalomaniac seeks wider scope for his activities.

MORIARTY

I reiterate my point. Do you take it?

HOLMES

If you are a megalomaniac, you are not a criminal. You are a megalomaniac, therefore you–

MORIARTY

Q.E.D. I am not a criminal.

HOLMES

Then, how do you explain your ever present hand in all these criminal operations, not to mention this little murder of Admiral Kovalevsky?

MORIARTY

There is, it seems to me, a fairly obvious explanation.

HOLMES

I should be delighted to hear it.

MORIARTY

I rather thought you could solve the puzzle without my assistance. You disappoint me, Mr. Holmes. Obviously I am into criminal activity for legitimate purposes.

HOLMES

You mean that–

MORIARTY

The truth is obvious, isn't it?

HOLMES

Then, for years I've ignored the most obvious signs.

MORIARTY

Your humble servant, Mr. Holmes. A government, any government, must have a means of performing certain necessary acts that it can later disown. Now for that a professional network is usually created. But for some activities auxiliaries are required. You see before you the Commander of Her Majesty's Auxiliary Forces.

HOLMES

Preposterous!

MORIARTY

I hold the rank of Brigadier in the Service. My immediate superior is M, the Head of Her Majesty's Secret Service.

HOLMES

Preposterous!

MORIARTY

You grow repetitious, my dear fellow. As it happens, you know M quite well. But you know him better as your brother Mycroft.

Enter Mycroft Holmes, large, sleek, fat, unlike the wiry Sherlock.

MYCROFT

It's true, Sherlock. Professor Moriarty is an agent of the Queen. I might add, a man who has proved himself indispensable on many occasions.

HOLMES

And, does Her Majesty see fit to employ murderers?

MYCROFT
(complacently)

Occasionally. But we don't consider this to be
murder. Admiral Kovalevsky was a military target.
Kovalevsky was a chief of the Okhrana and one of
the most effective Russian agents in Europe. He was
responsible for torturing and murdering several of our
best people. Therefore, Her Majesty's Government
decided to pay him quits. Moriarty handles delicate
matters like these for us. And very well.

END OF FLASHBACK. The lights blackout, then go up on
Holmes and Watson.

HOLMES

So you see, Watson, even the best detectives can
make mistakes. For years, I had tracked Moriarty
only to find out I was tracking my own brother,
whose commands Moriarty faithfully executed. And
that was why the Professor always eluded me, despite
my best efforts. Always, there was an impediment,
unforeseen, unforeseeable. I suspected he had
protectors in high places–but how high, how high...
The man Moriarty employed to kill the Admiral
thought he was performing a simple robbery for a
master criminal. He hadn't the slightest notion he was
working for Her Britannic Majesty.

WATSON

But none of this explains the pictures, Holmes. How
could you do such a thing?

HOLMES

What on Earth are you talking about? What pictures?

WATSON

The pictures of Irene Adler.

HOLMES

I know nothing of any pictures of Irene Adler. Bye the bye, she looked charming tonight.

WATSON

You saw her?

HOLMES

She wanted my cab, but I told her I was engaged.

WATSON

Did she recognize you?

HOLMES

Of course not. Now, what about these pictures?

WATSON

Holmes, how could you do such a thing–even for Queen and Country?

HOLMES

Watson, are you mad? What are you talking about?

Irene Adler has come in through the half open door. Suddenly, she lurches towards Holmes with a stiletto.

WATSON

Holmes, look out!

HOLMES

I have her, Watson.

IRENE

I will kill you yet, if I live. You will pay for what you did to me–for what you did to my husband.

HOLMES

Frau Adler, or I should say Mrs. Norton, I have no idea what you are talking about. Please calm yourself.

IRENE

Calm myself? After you blackmailed me to become a spy and then caused my husband to commit suicide. That will calm me?

HOLMES

I implore you to be calm. The last time I saw you or your husband was on your wedding day.

IRENE

Do you hear him, Dr. Watson, this liar? If you are a gentleman, Dr. Watson, you will help me to avenge myself.

Watson stands irresolute.

HOLMES
(perceiving Watson's confusion)
Watson?

WATSON
(coming to a decision)
Frau Adler, I believe you were injured by someone. But, but, I know this is Sherlock Holmes, and I know he is not the man who injured you.

HOLMES

Thank you, Watson. Now, Mrs. Norton, will you explain?

WATSON

This poor, gallant woman has been blackmailed by a man purporting to be you, Holmes.

HOLMES

Blackmailed! To do what?

IRENE

To spy and to become the mistress of the King of Bohemia.

HOLMES

What? Look carefully at me, Mrs. Norton. Are you sure I am the person who blackmailed you?

IRENE

If it was not you, it was someone who resembled you greatly. I am no longer sure. There are certain subtle differences.

HOLMES

It was Moriarty. I am sure of it.

IRENE

But, why would this Moriarty, whoever he is, describe himself as you?

HOLMES

The better to gain your initial confidence. Oh, he is a wonderful villain.

WATSON

But, Holmes, you just told me he works for your
brother Mycroft on special service.

HOLMES

That makes him no less a scoundrel. For that matter,
Mycroft is a scoundrel, if you come right down to it.
Nothing would please Moriarty more than to blacken
my name. Mrs. Norton, have you been victimized?

Enter Professor Moriarty dressed as Sherlock Holmes.

MORIARTY
(in a voice almost identical to Holmes')
You are quite right. I took the liberty of entering
without knocking when I saw Mrs. Norton come in.
Do you approve of my disguise, Mr. Holmes?

HOLMES

Moriarty, you will answer to me for this deception.

MORIARTY

Tsk, tsk. I am under orders, my dear Sherlock. Take
it up with your brother.

HOLMES

You mean, my brother authorized you to employ my
name in a blackmail scheme?

MORIARTY

I confess I did suggest it myself.

HOLMES

Devil!

MORIARTY

But he approved it. Calm down. Sherlock, you look
as though you'll have apoplexy. We mustn't lose a
great mind like yours to anger.

HOLMES

Why have you come here?

MORIARTY

I have some instructions for Mrs. Norton.

IRENE

I no longer take orders from you.

MORIARTY

Please, don't make it necessary for me to remind you
of the consequences of disobedience.

IRENE

I no longer take orders from you.

MORIARTY

Do not be childishly stubborn. You have no choice.

IRENE

I don't care. My husband is dead. You cannot
threaten me.

MORIARTY

Your husband was murdered.

IRENE

What do you say?

WATSON

Murdered? But he was a suicide?

HOLMES
Did you murder him, Moriarty?

MORIARTY
Me? No. What on Earth for? I needed him to keep
Mrs. Norton in line. But I know who did.

IRENE
(icily, but with restrained hysteria)
Who murdered my husband?

MORIARTY
Why, the King of Bohemia, of course.

IRENE
Why should he do that? I don't believe it.

MORIARTY
Your husband, Alfred Norton, was hired by the King
about the same time he engaged Sherlock Holmes.
The King is not a complete fool. Norton was engaged
to marry you and keep you quiet, a job he succeeded
in admirably. Holmes was assigned the rather more
simple task of obtaining the photograph. Norton was
the King's real trump. The King believes in having
more than one string to his bow.

IRENE
I don't believe it.

MORIARTY
Oh, I think I shall convince you. Norton had
instructions to kill you if you should continue in your
attempts to expose His Majesty.

IRENE
Not Alfred. He was so kind.

MORIARTY

No, not Alfred Norton. The man you married under
that name was Saladin, also known as the Marquis
Franz de Rosenthal, a ruthless and cunning French
criminal, nicknamed the "Sword Swallower." He was
once the leader of the notorious Black Silk Hoods
gang of Paris–a man of a thousand faces, you know.

IRENE

No.

MORIARTY

Do you know where your husband obtained his
income from?

IRENE

He had some money that he– Oh, it's true. His money
always came from Bohemia.

HOLMES

Why did the King kill Norton, or Saladin, then?

MORIARTY

After the King resumed his affair with Mrs. Norton,
he felt Saladin's services were superfluous. Moreo-
ver, Saladin was in a position to blackmail the King.
It's not the first time the King has paid off his agents
in that coin.

IRENE

(dejectedly)

And I thought there was one man who loved me for
myself alone.

HOLMES
(constrainedly)
Perhaps there is, Frau Adler, but it is not your
husband.

IRENE
Nonetheless, what has been done to me is despicable.

MORIARTY
Agreed. But would it not be more despicable to
permit a World War to break out when the means are
at hand to prevent it? Those photographs which
turned up when we disposed of Admiral Kovalevsky
gave us the opportunity to place an agent of influence
in the highest quarters of the country we call
Bohemia. We could not turn our backs on that opportunity. Will you continue to work for us? I ask
you in the name of all Mankind.

Irene hesitates and looks to Sherlock Holmes who remains
impassive.

MORIARTY
I wish to return these photographs to you, Madame.
Your work is too important to be continued under du-
ress.

IRENE
I will do so, and willingly.

MORIARTY
I regret the necessity that forced me to play the part
of a villain. The fate of the world rests on your success.

IRENE
(majestically)
War will not break out if it lies in my power to prevent it.

She shakes hands all around and walks out proudly.

WATSON
Magnificent creature!

MORIARTY
A real heroine. Well, my dear Sherlock, I'd better be going. Pleasant seeing you again.

HOLMES
One thing before you go, Professor.

MORIARTY
Anything for you, sir.

HOLMES
The photographs, if you will.

MORIARTY
What photographs?

HOLMES
Why, the ones you did not return to Mrs. Norton. Now give them here, Professor, or I shall put a bullet in your unscrupulous brain. I should hate to deprive Her Majesty of your so useful services.

CURTAIN

ABOUT THE TRANSLATOR

Frank J. MORLOCK is an accomplished translator and has translated numerous plays by Alexandre Dumas including *Hamlet, Dr. Sturler's Experiment* (epilogue to *Comte Hermann*), *Napoleon Bonaparte, The Musketeers, The Barricades of Clichy, Lorenzino, The Vampire* a.k.a. *The Return of Lord Ruthven* (published by Black Coat Press), *Le Vingt-quatre février, Antony, La Reine Margot, Caligula, Urbain Grandier, Monte-Cristo, The Whites and the Blues, The Youth of Louis XIV, Kean* and many others.

Frank has also translated Victor Hugo's dramas, *Les Miserables, Ninety Three, Hans of Iceland* and *Notre-Dame de Paris* (to be published by Black Coat Press in *Frankenstein Meets The Hunchback of Notre-Dame*) as well as numerous other plays such as Charles Nodier's *The Vampire* (published by Black Coat Press in *Lord Ruthven the Vampire*), *Madame Aubin* by Verlaine and *Signora Fantastici* by Madame de Stael. He also had three plays published by Rogue Publishing: Dumas' *The Man in The Iron Mask*, Victorien Sardou's *Young Figaro* and Maurice Leblanc and François de Croisset's original *Arsène Lupin*.